HAVING FAITH

MATURE LOVE SERIES

Georgia Tingley

Georgeous

Publishing

Cover design – Danielle Maait

Editing/Proofreading – KD Proofreading

www.georgiatingley.com

#9780648267577 - EPUB

#9780648267560 - MOBI

#9780648267584 – PRINT

ACKNOWLEDGEMENTS

I didn't realise until the time came to acknowledge my beta-readers, how many have actually had input into what worked and what didn't. So, thank you, one and all for your awesome thoughts. – Ruby Smith, Beanice Tyrrell, Genelle Jones, Mary Kovacevich, Carolyn Lamac, Tracey Perry, Dannielle Line, Jillian Jones, Cynthia MacLean, Lelia Higgins and Sheri Olson.

DEDICATION

As always, I dedicate my stories to my husband Colin,
who has intricately twined his fingers and heart with
mine. It's the best feeling in the world.

HAVING FAITH

FAITH –

When my best friend suggested I take a young, hot, sexy, stud-muffin as my date to meet my ex-husband's much younger fiancée, I allowed my arm to be 'twisted.' Nudging Forty, I felt battered, and my ego bruised - it was just what I needed.

"Who do you have in mind?"

"*Adam,*" Rachel voiced the one name hovering between us since the words, *sexy, hot,* and *young,* had been mentioned in the same sentence.

Adam was my friend's younger half-brother. We'd always been close, and I'd considered him to be a young brother to myself as well. Then something unthinkable happened between us on his eighteenth birthday that drove him away for ten years.

Now he was back, looking so good it should be illegal, and wanting to resume where we had left off. The soul-incinerating chemistry still bound us, but was my self-doubt too big a hurdle to leap?

ADAM -

For the longest time, Faith has been perched on the

peripheral edges of my heart. Since that fated night all those years ago, I had known she was it for me. I was a boy then, too young and dumb to understand that we were soulmates. But my heart knew it, and never let me forget. I'd tried to move on, I really had. She was married, after all.

So, when my sister asked if I could do Faith a favour and play along as her date to meet her idiot ex-husband and his soon-to-be trophy wife, I knew fate was opening a door for me.

This time, I was no amateur. This time, all I had to do was convince her we were meant to be. Sounds easy, right? Well, you haven't met Faith!

HAVING FAITH

1

Faith

Robert is getting married!

The words sunk in, at the grocery store of all places. I stared at row upon row of dog food, everything from dry biscuits, to tins of meat 'recommended by top-breeders'. Ironic really. I didn't even own a dog. But this was where the shocking news, which my ex-husband announced via a text message an hour earlier, had hit home.

A still functioning part of my brain registered I was receiving odd looks from people shopping. I was blocking their view and their access to the canned goods. Somehow, it didn't motivate me to move, which annoyed one harassed looking mother who pushed my shopping cart out of the way.

I turned my gaze and looked at her with blank eyes, before wandering up the aisle, zombie-like, pushing the cart with my hips. Clutching my mobile in my hand, I glared at the text on the screen, my mind a jumble of thoughts crowding in at once.

Now I blocked the cat food section.

Shoving my phone into my handbag, I gazed unseeing at the packets of meat on the shelf. It shouldn't surprise me. Hadn't Scott mentioned his dad was seeing a woman who worked in his office? She'd been over for dinner last weekend. What did he say her name was? I tapped my red varnished fingernail against my chin in thought. Shoniqua... Sheena... Shakira... One of those ridiculous names reserved for popstars.

"Excuse me, are you going to buy anything, or just stand there and stare at the boxes?"

Snapping out of my dazed state, I smiled at the same woman who'd pushed my trolley aside moments ago. A dirty-faced toddler sat in the seat of her shopping cart, and two school-aged kids in uniform stood next to her. They smirked at her sarcastic question, while she threw me a filthy look.

My face grew hot. "Oh, sorry. I was miles away."

I tossed boxes of cat food into my cart before wheeling it out of her way, grabbing a packet of dry biscuits one-handed as I maneuvered around her.

A baby, two kids, a dog, and a cat, too - no wonder you're so uptight, I grouched under my breath. I looked back at the little family. Oh, I was mean, she had her hands full, I guess she deserved some slack.

I rolled the trolley as far away from the annoyed customer as I could and ended up in the dairy section. A chill moved up my spine. The cotton summer dress I'd slipped on this morning was fine outside in the humid Queensland day, but in the shopping centre, the combination of the efficient air conditioning system and refrigerated shelves left me feeling cold. Goosebumps stood out on my arms and I shivered. Perhaps it had more to do with my thoughts rather than with the cool atmosphere.

I'd always expected Rob and I would reunite someday. It was one of my most consistent fantasies: he'd come crawling back, begging for forgiveness, exclaiming he 'couldn't live without me,' and I'd graciously accept ... or not.

Well, now it's just a stupid fantasy. Rob's text had rudely yanked me into reality.

The bastard.

As strange as it seemed, I expected to be more hurt. More bruised. But all I felt was a jarring sensation of disorientation, like being trapped in an episode of The Twilight Zone. Maybe I was too shell-shocked to sense any pain? It would explain the lack of emotion.

"Whoa."

I glanced at my watch and frowned in irritation. I'd been so lost in my thoughts for the last twenty minutes analysing this new state-of-affairs and my reaction, now I was running late. I'd have to hurry if I wanted to get to the bank before it closed.

Racing around the shop, I threw things into the trolley, pulling up at the sales counter seconds in front of a tall man. I suffered a flash of guilt with my almost-full cart of shopping, especially when his minuscule amount barely met the twelve items or less express checkout lane. Which he should be in anyway, I thought crossly. A quick glance over confirmed the long queue. No doubt it's why the poor man chose to stay behind me.

I'm running late, I justified to myself, avoiding eye contact so I wouldn't feel obligated to let him go first. After all, he has the opportunity to use the self-help checkouts.

After placing the dividing bar onto the conveyor belt, I bent to unload my shopping. I sensed his gaze burning into my back and his close scrutiny on the edges of my peripheral vision but continued to unpack my groceries. I faced the other direction, doing my best to ignore him while waiting for the woman in front of me to pay the cashier so I could retrieve the remaining items.

If he was expecting an apology or even an acknowledgment of his much smaller load, he'd be waiting a long time. My thoughts were uncharitable in my haste. But that wasn't what was on his mind.

"Do you need a hand, Faith?" a deep, masculine voice asked.

I stiffened. *That voice.*

Strong, capable, darkly tanned hands reached into my shopping cart and started to stack things on the conveyor belt, which now moved forward.

I spun around and stared into a wide, light-grey cotton covered chest. My gaze travelled upward to zero in on the most beautifully intense navy-blue eyes. Recognition, and something else I was reluctant to name, zinged down my spine, making my legs go weak.

"Oh my God, Adam. I'm so sorry. I didn't know it

was you. I'm in such an obscene hurry. I raced in and ..." I broke off to stop my babbling.

Sometimes when I was nervous, I babbled. Of course, I wasn't nervous now; I was just ... thrown. Catapulted more like it. To see this boy, make that 'man', from my past.

Adam was my best friend's half-brother. Rachel and I had spent a good portion of our teen years babysitting him. And although a ten-year age gap existed between us, we'd been extremely fond of each other, and the friendship continued even after I'd married.

But then something embarrassing happened. A night when everything changed forever. And I hadn't seen him since.

"All the more reason to help."

His words pulled me back to the present with a jolt.

"Look, there's not much left. Why don't you pack, and I'll unload?" he suggested with a smile; one of those endearing, lopsided grins I remembered from when he was a kid. Only, they didn't make my stomach do somersaults back then.

I took a deep calming breath, reluctant for his assistance. Especially when I looked at the remaining items in the trolley and winced to spot a packet of sanitary napkins proclaiming what time of the month it was for me. A wobbly smile of acceptance pulled at my mouth, and grabbing my reusable cloth bags, I handed them to the young salesgirl. Shuffling out of the way to the end of the benchtop, I rummaged in my handbag pretending to search for my wallet.

Stealing glances at Adam as he unloaded my shopping, I examined his sure, economical movements. I couldn't help but notice the tight, lean lines of his denim clad butt, and his powerful legs tapering downward to classic Adidas joggers. The salesclerk stopped packing and scanning, and instead joined me, both of us running our gazes over him when he leaned in to collect the last item.

We snapped to attention when he swivelled to place it on the conveyor belt. The sales-assistant gave the other girl on the next counter a hard stare until she, too, resumed work.

Holy shit, Rachel never told me how hot he was now.

"Just how many cats have you got, Faith?"

"Oh." I gave my head a slight shake, snapping out of my lust trance.

Looking down at the boxes sitting on the conveyor belt, heat suffused my cheeks, realizing too late the amount I'd hurled into the trolley in my haste to escape the sarcastic woman.

"Only the one," I mumbled, giving a lame excuse. "But he's a pig and has a monster appetite. I don't like to run out because he's such a nag when it comes to food. I'm worried he might gnaw on my foot when I'm asleep."

I babbled again.

We laughed together as we hadn't done in years and it felt good. Better than good actually, it reminded me of old times, and a wave of nostalgia hit in my chest.

After paying the salesgirl, I turned awkwardly to Adam. The empty shopping cart stood between us, I still needed to load my groceries into it.

"Well ..."

My words of goodbye died as Adam leaned over my trolley toward me. I inclined forward for his farewell kiss, a slight pout on my mouth, but to my horror, he bent into the cart to retrieve a small tin of tuna he'd missed.

Pulling back, my face flamed hot. I stole a look over at the salesgirl self-consciously. Her lips twisted, holding back a smirk.

Fuck.

"Sorry, must have missed this."

He held the can out in the palm of his hand to show me. I stared at it, lost for words. My traitorous eyes slid over his beautifully long-fingered hand, and my dirty mind conjured up images of those fingers stroking me. Images best forgotten.

Sheesh, I really needed to get laid.

"I'll put it in with mine," he offered at my mute response.

Pulled out of my sensual daydream, I nodded absently, feeling foolish. Twisting, I lifted my bags into the now empty trolley and chided myself for my thoughts. I'd totally lost the plot today. Now, instead of the quick getaway I'd planned, I had to wait for my stupid tin of tuna.

I waited impatiently at the end of the counter for Adam to pay for his shopping and my fish, taking the opportunity to reacquaint myself with his looks. He wore his almost-black hair shorter than the last time I'd seen him, which was years ago when he'd been a teenager, and the lead singer of a wannabe rock band. Cropped around his face and longer on the top, it looked finger combed into a tousled, take your breath away style.

His dark blue eyes, framed by thick sooty lashes which should be illegal for a man to possess, were vivid, and by far his best feature. They'd always been too gorgeous and placed him in the male super-model category in my mind.

Unaware of my furtive scrutiny, he turned and dropped the offending tin into one of my reusable bags. I pushed my trolley away from the bench and swung around to face him. He was standing close. Too close.

"I ... thanks for your help, but I've ... gotta ..."

My words dropped away. Our eyes met and held. I lost my train of thought. I had to go someplace, and it was quite urgent. But where?

We both stood staring at each other, enclosed in this bubble of mutual fascination. I watched as his eyes inched over my face, and I worried he'd note the changes the years had wrought and be disappointed.

I prayed I hadn't chewed off the pale pink lip-gloss I'd applied earlier, or my once neatly styled hair, which I'd raked back into a tidy top knot this morning, wasn't as flyaway as it felt. Self-conscious under his scrutiny, I pushed the wispy bits back into place and licked my dry lips.

His gaze was slow, drawn to my now moist lips, which made my mouth dry up even more. Was it my imagination, my shameful wishful thinking, or did he look at them with a hungry intensity? I swallowed thickly, seeking eye contact to confirm my crazy thoughts, but he was smiling now, in a casual off-handed way. The smile you'd give an acquaintance.

Okay, it's official. I'm going insane.

"Do you want to grab a drink? You know, to catch up on old times?"

His tone sounded hesitant and unsure, the complete opposite of how confident and comfortable he looked.

Oh, how I'd love that. My heart leapt and beat a rapid tattoo at the idea. But I dare not. What if he brought up the incident?

Recalling that night would be too awkward and embarrassing. And how could we not remember it? Even now, it sat uncomfortably between us, like an unwanted parent on a first date. My face grew warm again, simply from the memory. No, I couldn't, it would be unbearable.

"No," I blurted aloud, cutting him off as he was about to say something further, and drawing the attention of the salesgirl standing a few feet away. I looked around self-consciously, throwing a sheepish grin to the girl.

"What I ... I mean is," I stuttered like a jumpy adolescent. "I really ... I'm late. Maybe another time?"

A closed expression stole over his features.

"No problem, Faith. Good to see you again."

He stepped around me and walked away, throwing a casual backhanded wave.

"I ... it was good to see you too, Adam," I called out, my voice sounding breathy and lame, much to my dismay.

I felt hurt at his quick dismissal, which was crazy since I'd been the one to decline his offer. Well, what did I expect? After the way I had rejected him in the past, and now, rebuffing his reconciliatory gesture.

He must think I'm a bitch.

Adam sauntered away toward the exit and I grimaced, noticing how his loose-limbed, athletic stride drew many admiring and lustful gazes from women of all ages.

Hmm, nothing's changed there.

Dejected, I started to push the cart out to my car, automatically glancing back to check if I'd left anything on the counter. The salesgirl caught my eye, giving me a 'you blew it' look. I promptly looked away.

I did 'blow it', I grumbled to myself.

I struggled to steer my loaded trolley onto the uneven paving outside. Of course, it developed a mind of its own, and refused to go in the direction I wanted. It was karma; the universe was sending me a message - *That's for being so mean to such a sweet guy.'*

After loading the car and pushing the unwieldy trolley into the cart corral, I slid into the hot seat and snapped the seatbelt into place. I looked down at the face of my watch and sighed in frustration, it was one of those days when I should have stayed in bed. The bank was now closed.

Bending forward, I rested my head on the steering wheel. Hot tears pricked in my eyes. I blanched as the memory from that fateful night made a subliminal guest appearance. Determined, I shoved it back into its subconscious corner and dragged my thoughts back to the present.

I hadn't seen Adam in eleven years. Boy, he'd sure grown up in the interim. I'd forgotten how tall he was. Standing at five-ten myself, I looked many men in the eye, or sometimes, even down on them. Today however, I'd tilted my head back just to eyeball the man. He had to be at the very least, six-two. He must have been tall years ago, but his chest and shoulders were filled out, making him appear even bigger. But for all his height and size, he was lean. Built with not an ounce of fat, an athlete's body; a runner or a tennis player.

I looked downward at my tummy, still flattish, but a

little pouch had developed.

Shit. I should hit the gym.

A lone tear slid down my cheek. I scrubbed it away and gave myself a dressing down.

"Don't fucking cry. That's all you need, Faith," I muttered the words aloud in my locked car. "What with Rob getting married, seeing super-hot Adam and then promptly screwing it up, on top of getting your period, and putting on weight; the last thing you want is to have a one-person pity party."

I turned the key in the ignition. "Kill me now, aargh!"

2

Adam

Sliding behind the wheel of my dark SUV, I pulled the seatbelt over my shoulder. My back pocket vibrated against my butt.

"Shit."

It had turned into an annoying habit of mine, getting into my car and forgetting my mobile in my pocket. Climbing out of the car, I pressed the answer button and held it to my ear.

"Where are you?" my half-sister Rachel barked, without giving me the chance to even say a greeting.

"Hey, Rach."

My sister asked me to buy a few groceries for dinner

at her place tonight. It was a family affair, celebrating my return to the Sunshine State. For the past ten years I'd lived in Perth, Western Australia, as far away from Faith as I could go; to get over of my infatuation with her.

It didn't work.

So, I returned home to Townsville. I'd missed the tropical climate, and it felt good to experience again the sticky, warm air from my childhood.

With our folks and younger sibling, Monique, Rachel's husband, two girls, and Monique's boyfriend in attendance, the party had grown, hence the trip to the shops. The urgency of the food slipped my mind after bumping into Faith. It was just as well she'd turned down my invitation for drinks.

"Oops, sorry Rach, I ran into an old friend. On my way."

"Break the land speed record if you have to. I need that cream."

Chuckling, I hung up and slipped into my seat, tossing my phone onto the passenger side. In the process of turning the engine over, I glimpsed Faith a few metres away in the other parking aisle. She packed the last of her shopping into the boot of her car, so engrossed in her actions, she hadn't seen me.

She must have passed when I was speaking to Rachel and facing the other direction. My unfamiliar car didn't elicit a glance from her when depositing her empty trolley in the cart bay.

A brisk sea-breeze which picked up in the last hour, plastered her dress against her body, outlining her shape, while the bulk of material flapped behind. The thin fabric moulded to her breasts, drawing attention to the two perfect, hand-sized mounds. Her peasant blouse style sleeve had fallen off one shoulder, revealing a black bra strap as she wrestled with the shopping cart in the strong wind, a dickey wheel making the task even more humorous to watch. She pushed it into the corral and kicked the offender for good measure.

A grin twisted my lips at the sight. It was so Faith.

The tightening of my jeans was a sure sign my reaction to her hadn't changed over the years. The fact watching her was all it took was worrying though. That hadn't changed either. I had always been on the outside watching her.

Geez, get a grip, Warner.

I smiled at the thought but didn't look away.

Faith still had an exquisite body, slender, with curves in the right places. A cute butt, and long tanned legs, which seemed to go on forever. I liked the fact she was tall. She could have become a model with no effort if she hadn't got mixed up with such an asshole and become pregnant so young. Her life would have been so different if she hadn't met and married Robert Newman.

At least she'd followed her dream and become a beautician who ran her own moderately successful business. When I left, she'd worked for someone else. I made it a point to keep in touch, if not personally, then at least through my sister. If it was up to me, I would have kept in contact, but Faith made it abundantly clear she didn't want anything to do with me. In fact, she'd gone out of her way to avoid me - and I had missed her.

Just how much I'm only now starting to realize.

Oh, but she looked so good. I wanted to drink her up, absorb every last drop of all the little changes time made to her.

Her golden brown hair had darkened over the years, and although it remained mostly hidden pinned up on top of her head, I loved the way little strands refused to be tamed, and broke free of their confinement to curl around her face. I could tell she found it annoying. I found it delightful.

It did, however, draw attention to her slender and graceful neck. I had a thing about women's necks. I loved the long swooping lines, the delicate artistry. Loved to burrow my face, stroking and kissing my way down their throat, inhaling their fragrance, and feeling the little pulse beating in the hollow. Faith's neck was beautiful; pale and fine-boned.

She was my 'Michelle Pfeiffer' growing up. Maybe not in the petite way the actress was, but she possessed the same heart-shaped face and high rounded cheekbones, surrounded by riotous honey coloured hair.

Today I'd wanted to memorize every feature and store it away for later recall. In particular, her eyes, always the colour of warm honey, they hadn't changed. Cat's eyes, she called them. I'd never come across another person with the same golden shade.

Considering the stress her husband put her through since the separation and divorce, she still looked remarkably youthful. Her skin, still smooth and pale, and the splash of freckles across the bridge of her cute, perky nose gave her an adolescent appearance. She'd always been paranoid about them, hiding them under copious amounts of foundation, and protecting her skin from the sun's rays long before it was fashionable or health conscious to do so. But they always seemed to bleed through by the end of the day.

Her obsession with wearing baseball caps had certainly paid off; her skin looked flawless.

I could have studied her for hours. Only her sudden stillness, giving away her wariness, forced me to smile casually. Difficult to do, given what I truly wanted, was to wrap my arms around her and crush her against me, pull the pins out of her hair and bury my face into the fragrant essence of Faith.

If I had my way, I'd have grabbed her hand and taken her home to make love all night long. I smirked. 'Making love'. It sounded too tame for what I wanted to do with Faith. What I felt. What I'd always felt, was something wild and powerful, and so much more.

I shifted restlessly on the leather seat and fantasized about what I would do. For starters, I'd watch her hair tumble around her shoulders to curl around her face in wild abandon. I longed to slide the bodice of her peasant blouse down, baring her to the waist with the need to see and touch her warm, naked body.

But most of all, I wanted to kiss her. To take up where we left off those many years ago. To kiss her, taste her, and immerse myself in her. And then ... I wanted to start over again.

I'm like a randy teenager.

I snickered. It surprised me.

Although why the hell that was, I didn't know. She'd always made me feel this way. Only back then, I 'had' been a randy teenager.

For fuck's sake, would it never change with her?

Well, at least seeing her today had confirmed one

thing in my head. The fascination I had for Faith remained strong still; and now, I knew I had to do something about it. What that something was, though, was more problematic to define. I couldn't leave it alone. Not this time. Not now that she's a single woman.

I could no longer discount the chemistry existing between us, as I had been doing for the last eleven years. They needed exploring. If it was nothing but sexual, well we'd have a bloody good time as long as it lasted. I'd finally be able to get her out of my system. But if it turned out to be something more ... it definitely needed further examination.

This time around there were no obstacles standing in our way. No husband. No wife. No small child. The biggest stumbling block I might foresee was Faith herself.

She'd always held so many preconceived ideas about what was correct and what wasn't. The age difference would be a big one for sure. I needed to remind her these days more and more men were choosing older women as partners.

In years past, it was thought women over thirty had passed their use by date. But these days, we consider women in their thirties and even forties to be in their prime, sexy and desirable. And no woman had ever appealed to me on as many levels as Faith did. I didn't care about her age, and I wasn't about to let her use that as an excuse.

Faith's head bent down to rest on her arms, which she'd folded over her steering wheel. I leaned forward in my seat, peering across the car park.

Was she crying?

An overriding urge to protect came to the fore. Perhaps I shouldn't interfere, but all I knew was Faith needed me. Climbing out and locking my car, I made my way over to her.

Before I'd gone two steps, Faith had lifted her head and started the ignition. I stood transfixed in the middle of the parking lot, and watched as she reversed and drove out, without even seeing me in her rear vision mirror.

You're not driving out of my life this time, Faith. This time I'm gonna have you.

The words, although said under my breath, were a promise to myself I intended to keep.

3

Faith

"**I** think you should take a sexy, young, gorgeous stud muffin, and introduce him to Rob as your lover."

"You think I should what?" I spun away from the kitchen counter to stare open-mouthed at the woman sitting calmly at my breakfast bar.

"You heard me, Faith. Why don't you go to the dinner party with a gorgeous younger man of your own?" Rachel snickered.

Rob was insisting I meet his bride-to-be before they got married. Since our lives would crossover for family events, he reasoned it would be better if everyone was on favourable terms. As much as I wanted to, I couldn't argue with his logic.

"I heard you all right. I just can't believe you'd suggest such a thing."

"Why not, for heaven's sake? You have to go to the dreaded dinner, so why not take a date? After all, Scott's taking Michelle. Rob will have Miss Universe. So, you're left high and dry playing third wheel all night."

I screwed my face up at her words. She was right, of course. My heart sank at the thought of that happening.

"Hmm, good point. But doesn't it defeat the purpose of Rob seeing how hot I am and come running back to me? I don't want him to think I've moved on."

I turned back to spooning instant coffee into the two mugs on the stone countertop.

"Oh, for God's sake Faith, give it up."

My lips thinned, and I turned around once more, ready to tick off my friend.

"No, Faith."

Rachel's raised voice halted my words.

"It's time you let that stupid delusion go. It's not going to happen. And anyway, why do you want it to? He was an absent husband eighty percent of the time, and if you were truly honest with yourself, you'd admit you don't even have feelings for him anymore."

I opened my mouth to protest, then closed it again, then opened it once more as a thought crossed my mind, then closed it. I was doing a good impression of a fish out of water.

Rachel was right. I had given up on my so-called fantasy of Robert running back to me months ago. I enjoyed not having his daily criticism thrown in my face and wasn't as upset over his impending marriage as I thought I'd be. I wanted to confess as much to Rachel but held back. I needed time to scrutinize and dissect my reasons for having this change of heart. Something I hadn't allowed myself to do in the past year.

After the initial wedding announcement shock, all my mental attention seemed to be focused on another man the last couple of days. I pushed the thought aside. I would have to process that more as well.

"It's a good idea, Rach. The problem is, I don't know any sexy stud muffins. There's Scott's friend, Michael, and I draw the line at going out with my son's mate. All the other gorgeous young men I know are married - both of them," I joked, but in truth, I was being honest. I had kept away from men since two disastrous dates. Plus, until recently I'd always vaguely thought I'd get back with Rob.

Suddenly, a vision of the bluest eyes and dark, almost black hair, popped into my mind. I shook it away again, but the familiar crooked smile lingered.

Carrying the steaming mugs of coffee over, I placed them before my confidant. "I believe this conversation calls for cheesecake, don't you?"

"Oh, absolutely. We'll think much better on a full stomach. In fact, I've got someone in mind at this moment." Rachel gave a devious chuckle. "And if he agrees, your ex-husband better look out."

I hesitated while staring into the open refrigerator. I had a pretty good idea who Rachel had in mind. The accidental meeting, and now my friend's suggestion seemed too coincidental. I wondered if Adam had mentioned bumping into me. I hoped not since I felt guilty for not confiding in Rachel myself. I was planning on telling her today, but the whole Rob getting married thing sort of took precedence.

"What's wrong? Cheesecake gone green and furry?"

Brought back to reality by my companion's comments, I leaned in to pull out the plastic wrapped, strawberry-glazed cake.

"Bite your tongue. As if I'd allow cheesecake to go off. Not on my watch. And especially not in a house with a seventeen-year-old feeding machine." Slicing the cake and placing a large wedge before each of us, I bit the bullet and asked, "So, who did you have in mind?"

As if I didn't know.

I knew Rachel's mind almost as well as I knew my own. Not that that was a good reference. I didn't hold much confidence in knowing my own traitorous mind lately.

We'd been friends since preschool, living across the road from each other until I'd married and moved away. Even then, we'd see each other often, being more like sisters than friends. Our lives were so intertwined over the years, we often shared thoughts. Once again, those blue eyes popped into my head. Oh yeah, I knew for sure who Rachel had in mind before the words were even uttered.

"Adam."

She voiced the one name which had been hovering between us since the words, sexy, gorgeous, and young had been mentioned in the same sentence.

I sighed loudly, but before I could say a thing, Rachel rushed on.

"I know you'll say no. But what I don't understand is why not? Okay, so he kissed you. Come on Faith, it was ten years ago. He was eighteen at the time, and probably drunk and randy as hell. Plus, it was his birthday. Give the kid a break."

"Actually ..." I threw her an exasperated look. "What I intended to say was ... he was the first guy I thought of, too, unfortunately." I'd thought of very little else since our encounter two days earlier. "And for the record, it's been eleven years."

Rachel rolled her eyes at me.

Knowing my friend would not give up on this until I had given in, I groaned in acceptance of the truth.

"So, what is your darling brother doing back ... I mean these days?"

I held my breath hoping Rachel didn't realize the mistake I'd made. I shouldn't even know he'd returned.

"Cut the crap, Faith. He told me he met you the other day."

I pulled a face at my friend. "I planned to tell you."

Rachel threw a 'yeah right' look in my direction.

"I was. Honestly. If he told you already, I don't have much more to add. We bumped into each other at the grocery store. After a brief chat, he asked me to go for a drink with him and ..."

"Wait ... what?" Her high-pitched tone made me break off. Rachel glared at me. "He asked you to go for a drink?"

"Yeah," I said cautiously. I knew by her reaction I'd said something wrong, but I wasn't sure what it was. "But I said no, since I needed to get to the bank before it closed. But then I piss-farted around and didn't make it in time, anyway."

"Oh, the rat-bastard." Rachel scowled. "I was waiting for him to get back from the shop with cream for the potato-bake I'd prepared, and the whole time he was asking you to go out for a drink."

I cringed, biting my lip at my error and tried to defend him. "Well no, we didn't go for a drink because ..."

She cut me off.

"I know, Faith. But he would have. Typical Ads. He always did think the sun shined out of your ass."

I smiled and swivelled to look at my butt. "What? You mean it doesn't?"

Rachel looked daggers at me. Ignoring my joke, her hands lifted up, and she waved them in front of her as if wiping a chalkboard clean.

"Anyway, back to what we were talking about. What were we talking about?"

"I asked you what he was up to? Is he here on holiday?"

"Oh."

Rachel now had a guilty look, bending her head to hide her face in the fall of her smooth, shoulder-length blonde hair.

"I've been putting off telling you this, Faith, since I know how you feel about Adam. But, brace yourself. He's moved back."

"What? Why?" I snapped, my voice sounding far more alarmed than I had intended.

Rachel whipped her head up and glared at me. "Because this is his home. All his family are here."

I instantly felt terrible. "I'm sorry Rachel, of course it is. He has every right to live here. I'm sorry he thought I drove him away."

"No, you're not."

I opened my mouth in outrage at my friend's words.

"You know it suited you to not have him around,

making things awkward for you."

Her blue eyes narrowed on me.

I didn't say anything. What could I say? It was the truth. I blamed Adam for making things awkward, but the fact is, it was me. Now was not the time to analyse why. I'd take that home-truth out later to scrutinize.

"Well, what is he doing here? Has he got a job?"

Rachel seemed glad to continue on a lighter note.

"He's working with Cottrell & Laws, the builders."

I nodded. Adam was an architect, and I was glad he had returned to work for the same firm he did work experience with here in Townsville. They specialized in office buildings, and I remembered they valued his performance and promised him a job after he finished university. But he'd moved to Western Australia and never took them up on the offer.

Bringing the subject back to my date, I asked, "Do you think he'd agree to such a ridiculous request, or has he got himself a steady girlfriend who would object?"

I threw my question out casually, out of curiosity, of course. Nothing else.

"Uh-uh," Rachel mumbled over a mouthful of cake, shaking her head then swallowing. "He's always got a girl in tow, but nothing too serious, I don't believe."

"Well ... I don't know." I stalled and tried to come up with different excuses why Adam wouldn't be able to be my date. "He's probably too busy ... I mean an architect, for God's sake, he must be loaded down with work commitments. This is hardly important, after all. And anyway, he must be looking for someplace to live."

"Get real, Faith, surely you realise Adam would do anything for you? Rob knows him already. So, what if he goes as your date? Rob will jump to the conclusion you're lovers, especially taking into account 'the kiss' a few ..."

Rachel broke off, frowning at my shaking head.

"You mean you didn't tell him about 'the kiss'?"

"No." I chewed on my lip and grimaced in guilt. "I didn't think it wise to mention it. Rachel, the only person I even spoke to about it, is you. I don't know if Adam told anyone about it or not, but I'd pushed the incident to the back of my mind."

I felt foolish admitting the truth. Now she would know I'd made this into something much bigger than it should've been. Why hadn't I laughed it off?

Rachel's expression mirrored the exact thoughts ricocheting in my mind. "Okay, so why didn't you tell Rob? Surely you didn't think he'd be jealous?"

"No, of course not. I didn't tell him because ... well, just because, okay? Can we drop it?"

"Touchy. Methinks she protests too much." Rachel's eyes had a knowing look in them.

"Rach, can we get back on track here, and stop trying to analyse 'the kiss'." I made air quotes. "After all, as you said, the whole fiasco happened years ago."

I gathered up the dirty dishes, wanting to keep busy so Rachel couldn't look into my eyes, and see something I hadn't even come to terms with. "I haven't thought about that drama since, but now I have, don't you think it could make things a teeny bit awkward for us? I mean, I've obviously made this into a big deal, and I must admit, I've avoided Adam over the years, so much so, that now ... well, it's become an issue."

My cheeks grew warm, and I used the excuse of rinsing the dishes to hide my flaming face.

"If Adam even agrees to go," Rachel stated bluntly.

I turned from the sink to face my friend, throwing my arms up in the air in a dramatic gesture. I could feel my hair swinging around my face with my movements.

"What? So now you think he might not agree? What am I so worried for? He'll say no. Maybe he's even angry with me for not going with him for a drink. I don't understand, perhaps ..."

"He's not angry with you, Faith." Rachel interrupted my rambling. "I'm only messing with you."

"How do you know? Have you discussed me with him?" I turned accusing eyes on Rachel.

"No, not really. Not in any depth. He's asked, I've answered. End of story." She shrugged her shoulders dismissively.

I suddenly became very interested, leaning on the counter toward my bestie. "He's asked about me? What exactly?"

"Well, naturally, he asks after you out of polite curiosity ... every freakin' time we talk." She snorted. "He was particularly interested to hear you'd gotten divorced from 'dickhead'. He said he was going to call around to visit you, to cheer you up."

"Did you tell him Rob is getting married?"

Rachel looked at me as if I had gone insane. "You just told me today."

"Oh yeah, that's right, I did. Duh!" I was going mental. "You didn't text him when I went to the toilet, did you?" I looked at her in mock suspicion.

"Yep, you got me." Rachel jumped up from her seat and opened the pantry door. "Quick, hide. He's on his way over now."

We both laughed at her hilarious antics.

"Well, we'll never know what he's going to say unless

27

we ask him, right?" Rachel bent to scoop up her handbag off the tiled floor. "I'm going over to Mum and Pedro's tonight."

"Adam's in the process of moving into his own place, but he won't be in until next weekend, so I'll check out the situation with him and get back to you."

"How long has he been back?" I played with a serviette lying on the counter to make it look as though the question was a casual afterthought.

"About a month, I guess. Which is long enough for him to be over living with the folks."

"Huh … I'm glad I didn't hold my breath for him coming to visit me," I grumbled, pretending to examine a broken fingernail to hide the odd hurt feeling.

Rachel came over, giving me a big hug when she glimpsed a pained expression cross my face.

"He's going to say yes. You know Ads would do anything for you."

Her words brought a wobbly smile to my lips.

"And then you'll think 'what a great friend Rachel is', for suggesting I take him to the dinner."

Her comment brought a burst of laughter from me.

"I already think that, you dope." I pulled out of her arms, straightened up and wrapped my arms around her shoulders, giving her a big hug. "What did I do to have such a great person like you in my life?"

"Fuck knows."

I chuckled at her words but felt teary.

Rachel started to pull away, but I held on tight.

"Are you going to be okay?" she asked.

Being taller, my chin grazed her brow. I sniffed into her hair. "Yeah."

"Good, I'll text you tomorrow," she promised, before

pulling away and walking to the front door.

"No. Call me. You know I'll want to talk about it tonight." I made her agree while sauntering behind her down the hallway. "It doesn't matter how late you get in. I'll never sleep otherwise."

"Alright, but Steve won't like it. He thinks we should grow up and stop acting like fourteen-year-old schoolgirls."

I smiled at her husband's comments, knowing how he loved to stir us up.

"I hope you didn't let him get away with it?"

"Not bloody likely. I said I'll grow up when he stops playing computer games every chance he gets."

We threw our heads back and laughed. Rachel always had a good smart-ass comeback.

4

Faith

Night found me lying in bed anxiously awaiting Rachel's phone call. Glancing at the bedside clock, I sighed in exasperation; it was only ten minutes since the last time I checked. I read and re-read the same page of my book three times. It was no use. I couldn't do a thing until I'd heard from my friend one way or the other.

Rachel's crazy idea about taking Adam as my date had certainly taken my mind off my depressing thoughts. My mind flashed back to when things were much clearer and more defined in my relationship with my best friend's half-brother.

Rachel's mother, Julie, had remarried and started a family with her new husband, Peter Warner. When Adam was born, both Rachel and I, who were ten years-old at the time, adored him on sight as little girls do. We were always looking after him, especially when Julie gave birth to a girl two years later.

Being an only child, I'd longed for a little brother and soon developed a unique attachment to Adam. The feeling was reciprocated, and we soon formed a mutual admiration society between us.

I'd spent a lot of my youth looking after him. So much, on occasion I'd looked on Adam as a pesky little brother. Particularly when I was a teen, and he, an annoying and very naughty boy who always played pranks.

Throughout the years, Adam and I had a marvellous relationship, even after I met and married Rob and had my own son, Scott, when I was twenty-two. We still somehow remained close.

I leaned over to my bedside table and took a sip from the glass of scotch and dry I'd poured to fortify myself when I got the dreaded phone call from my bestie. I forced myself to relive what Rachel and I had named 'the kiss' incident.

Adam had always been a beautiful child with the light olive skin tone and dark hair he'd been blessed with from his father's Italian heritage. And those piercing blue eyes and cheeky grin were the cutest. In no time, he had grown to become a total hunk.

At only sixteen, he had to practically beat the girls off with a stick, not that I ever saw him trying. And at eighteen, he was drop-dead gorgeous. There were simply no other words to describe him. He should have been a male model or a movie star with his dark chocolate-brown scruffy hair, and overlong fringe which hung over his brow. His lean cheeks and defined square jaw covered in a light stubble, drew the eyes. He was tall, too, all lean male, even then.

If I had to point out one flaw, it was his crooked smile. But combined with his perfect white teeth, it was absurdly endearing and wrenched at my heart. It always had.

Adam continuously had girlfriends. As the lead-singer in a local rock band, girls were always phoning him or conveniently calling round for a visit. But Adam never let it go to his head. If anything, he seemed embarrassed by the female attention he received. For all his sex appeal, he was grounded and down to earth. And when he wasn't, Rachel and I soon burst his ego as only older sisters can.

They held his birthday party at his parents' home, still across from the house I'd grown up in. The Warner house was in an upmarket neighbourhood, the homes older and more established. Set on a big block, their property boasted lush tropical gardens with exotic plants and discreet lighting. The main body of the party was focused in the backyard which housed a lagoon style swimming pool.

The incident took place at the end of the night when the festivities started winding down. I'd been in the kitchen helping Rachel and her mother clean-up for the past hour and had decided it was time to go home. Most of the older relatives had long since retired for the night, and only a few of the hardier ones had stayed. Of course, it went without saying, the younger ones still partied on, and probably would until the very early hours of the morning.

Earlier, I had put Scott to sleep in Adam's bedroom. Now I went to wake him and attempt to carry him to the car. Shaking my six-year-old I whispered, "Come on buddy, we have to go home."

Scott opened sleepy eyes and mumbled, "Adam said I could sleep over tonight, Mummy. I'm gonna help him clean up in the morning."

I wondered if it was wise, but then considering there was a houseful of responsible adults, including Adam's parents whose bedroom sat across the hallway, I relented. Rachel and Adam's parents were like Scott's substitute grandparents, and he often spent the night at their place. Pulling the covers over him and gently kissing him goodnight, I left the lamp on, but turned down the dimmer switch in case Scott woke up in the night and worried where he was. But knowing my son, it seemed highly unlikely.

Next, I went looking for the birthday boy, wanting to say goodbye and once again wish him a happy birthday before I left.

I found him talking to some friends, and at my words he protested it was much too early for me to leave. Adam dragged me up onto the paved area which they'd been using as a dance floor, just as a slow, schmoozy, eighties number started to play.

Egged on by his mates, he pulled me into his arms, holding me close. Good-natured, I allowed myself to be held for a last dance. I was very aware of Adam in a man-woman kind of way; a way I wasn't used to thinking of my surrogate 'little brother'.

Held close to his warm body, my palms pressed flat on his chest. I was shocked to discover Adam's heart rate had picked up tempo as he danced. And even more shocked to discover mine had, too.

His hands glided down my bare arms, forcing my own to forsake their protective position. Leaving a trail of tingling warmth behind, he entwined his fingers intimately with mine, compelling our bodies into even closer proximity as we swayed in rhythm to the song.

My breasts rubbed against his chest, and I cringed inwardly as my betraying nipples hardened into beads easily felt through the thin material of my black halter party dress. It was the single, most-sexy thing a man had ever done to me on a dance floor.

We shuffled around, barely moving to the slow strains of the popular romantic ballad.

"You look beautiful tonight, Fate," he whispered into the hair at my temple. His breath blew warm, with the faint smell of alcohol.

"Thank you. You look pretty beautiful yourself, or maybe I should say handsome instead?" I didn't put too much meaning into his words at the time. Adam was always saying lovely things to me. Just as he always called me 'Fate', using his childhood name for me before he'd learned to pronounce my name correctly. Now, I questioned if perhaps I should have paid more attention to what Adam said.

Putting the glass to my lips, I took another sip from my scotch, then squirmed under the covers as the memories of the night started to arouse me. I recalled how the way he stared at me made me uncomfortable.

"I have to go, Adam. Scott's gone to sleep in your bed, and I have work in the morning."

"Relax, Faith. Scott's cool, and Rob's away for the weekend. Enjoy yourself." Releasing my hands, he pulled me possessively tighter into his embrace, wrapping his powerful arms around my narrow back.

"I don't think your girlfriend is going to like us dancing so close." I tried to appeal to his common sense.

He only shrugged, unconcerned he buried his nose in my neck. It felt so good in Adam's arms, better than good if I were to be perfectly honest, but at the same time, I became conscious of the odd looks we received from Adam's friends. His girlfriend looked as though she would throw a hissy-fit at any moment. I stiffened at my thoughts and tried to pull away.

Adam took a deep breath and released it before speaking. "Okay, okay. After this song fishes," he slurred a fraction. "I'll walk you out to your car."

"Fishes?" I laughed. "Is this song going fishing?" I teased him in an effort to lighten the mood, and he grinned good-naturedly, pulling me back into his arms.

"Thank you, Adam, but I don't want you to leave your friends. I'm sure I can manage to walk out to my car by myself."

With his promise, I now relaxed in his embrace and enjoyed the slow erotic movement of his hips against mine, closing my eyes to the surrounding censure. He was drunk, and the song was almost finished, I justified.

True to his word, after the song concluded, he insisted on carrying various items I had brought to the party out to my car in the driveway. After stowing them into the boot while I said my goodbyes in the house, Adam called me over to a darkened part of the front garden when I returned. Curious, I moved to where he stood amid an overgrown section of plants, a jungle type assortment of tree-sized tropical vegetation and huge ferns. Stepping over the native-violet ground cover onto strategically placed steppingstones, I found him leaning negligently against the thick wooden beam of the shade-cloth covered pergola.

"What's up?"

"Nothing much. I remembered you haven't given me a kiss for my birthday yet."

Although it was dark, I saw his eyes twinkling with mischief and his silly crooked grin starting to spread across his face. Deciding to play along with his game, knowing he had imbibed a little too much alcohol, I teased, "Are you sure? I could have sworn I gave you a huge, slobbery, suction-cup kiss when we first got here?"

"That," he chortled. "You call that a kiss."

He rolled his eyes and grabbed my hand, pulling me into his arms.

"It was a baby's kiss. I'm an adult now, remember? I need an adult to teach me how to kiss like an adult."

"Ha. You could probably teach me a thing or two ... or three, for that matter," I joked, still not realizing how serious he was.

His hungry eyes settled on my mouth and I had to swallow hard. "I don't think this is such a good ..."

"What's the matter, Fate? It's just one little kiss, and it is my birthday. Robert isn't here." He looked up and behind me, scanning the front garden. "Nobody's around to see, or to tell."

He was so persuasive, with his passionate eyes challenging me, daring me with a smouldering intensity I had never experienced before. And his mouth; sensitive and masculine, it curved in a sensual smile which stole my breath as I stared at it. His large hands moved to my waist and spread over my lower back, pulling me into his hips.

"Fate."

My eyes were drawn to his lips as they whispered my name. Even as I watched, his beautiful, sinful mouth came closer and closer, mesmerizing me.

"Oh, God."

I couldn't put up even a token resistance against the fierce surge of longing sweeping over me. Then his lips were on mine, and I tasted hunger and desire in his kiss. His hot mouth bore little resemblance to the polite 'baby' kisses I had exchanged with him practically my entire life. Instead, his caress was a man's - hard, intense, and forbidden.

This last thought fought its way to the surface through the lust clouding my brain, but Adam wouldn't allow it to break free. The intimate intrusion of his tongue was a fiery brand. He cupped my head with one hand, his other gliding down my back to settle on my backside, pressing me harder against his pelvis.

I kissed him back. Not because I wanted to, I convinced myself later, but because I couldn't help it. I'd known nothing like it before. At twenty-eight, it felt as though I'd never been kissed, which was ridiculous. I was a married woman, but he made me feel in all these years, I didn't know what kissing was about.

The most erotic and passionate sensations coursed through my body, and like a flash flood it engulfed me, shoving aside any resistance in its wake. His fierce longing transmitted to me with every stroke of his tongue.

He groaned softly into my mouth and pushed his

hips into my own. I felt his erection, hard, urgent, driving against me. My mind screamed at me to pull away. This was wrong.

Instead, without my permission, my hands moved to his head, my fingers sliding into his hair, and clutching at him as I deepened the kiss in hunger. Slanting my mouth over his and thrusting my tongue into his mouth, I tasted the heady flavour of bourbon as I now became the aggressor. I had never been so turned on in my entire life, not before then, and certainly not after.

Encouraged by my actions, Adam cupped my ass cheeks and pulled me into him. My dress was pushed up, so his hard cock now pressed against my damp panties as he ground against me.

Somehow, we reversed positions. I was now pressed against the brick wall of the house. With our mouths still fused together, his hand slid between us to cup my mound over my silky lingerie.

Pulling away, his lips moved to my neck. "I want you so much."

His voice rasped against my throat and I moaned, angling my head back to give him better access. His lips trailed a scorching path to my ear and he gently bit the lobe as his fingers slid beneath the silk.

"And you want me, too. You're so hot and wet."

His words, thick and breathless, whispered raggedly into my ear.

His long-fingered hands stroked and explored before sliding a finger inside me. I was so wound up with need, I almost came right then and there, but he lifted his head, and looked into my eyes with a fierce intensity.

"I want to watch you come for me."

I couldn't breathe at his words. Another finger joined the first and moved inside me, pumping in and out with a carnal rhythm.

"Ohh ..."

A whispered moan escaped my lips, and my hips picked up the cadence he set, driving wildly against his hand toward a climax. Holding myself still, I heard a small mewling sound come from me, before a jolt shuddered through my body as I arched into him. My eyes searched and held his before they closed in release, and I melted in his arms. I felt his head rest against mine and his lips move over my hair in a gentle brush.

Suddenly, the front door slammed shut as a young couple emerged from the house. We sprang apart, Adam pulling me discreetly back into the shadows of the fernery until they had walked off down the street.

"That was close."

His words brought me back to my senses, but then the horror of what had happened burst upon me. Pulling my clothes into order, anger washed over me. Anger at myself. Shocked I could feel this burning lust unfurling low in my belly for Adam. He was so young. Always like a little brother to me. And worst of all - I was a married woman whose husband was away.

Adam spoke in hushed tones, turning to face me. "Let's go to your place."

In shameful fury, I unleashed my rage on Adam instead. "How could you?" My harsh whisper echoed in the silence.

Disgusted with myself, I pushed past to stomp off. When he grabbed my arm and pulled me back into his embrace, I lost it, slapping him hard across his handsome face. I stood stunned at first to see the white imprint of my hand on his cheek. Then the harsh words came spewing from my lips. The regrettable words.

I cringed now in memory. Lying in bed, I buried my head in my pillow and groaned in embarrassment at the accusations I made.

"I trusted you, Adam. I'm married for God's sake." Not allowing him to get a word in, I continued. "Do you have to score with every woman you come across? Isn't half the female population in town enough for you? Next time you drink too much, don't come and see me."

I had a glimpse of Adam's hurt face but shoved the image to the back of my mind. In self-righteous indignation I strode purposely to my car and drove off, my hands shaking on the steering wheel, hot tears burning my eyes.

I hadn't seen Adam since.

I'd tortured myself continually over the following fortnight, picking up the phone countless times to apologize, but hanging up shortly after. Eventually, it went past the time for apologies, and I pretended as though nothing happened. For the entire year he was in Townsville, I somehow managed to avoid him.

I was guilt-ridden and remorseful. Although I took it out on Adam, my anger was self-directed. I was a married woman, and I'd behaved ... well, like a slut. I had almost ... I shuddered at the thought I couldn't even complete. I didn't even have the excuse of being drunk. Not even a tad inebriated. Since I planned to drive home with Scott, not a sip of alcohol crossed my lips.

I refused to think about it back then. Eaten up with guilt, I'd gone out of my way to try to make it up to Rob, never confessing to him what happened. Nor how aroused I'd been.

At last, in sheer self-preservation, I confided in Rachel, a watered-down version, which she brushed aside as of no account. Even Adam, she said, was acting normal. I prayed he'd gotten so shit-faced drunk he didn't remember it.

"You fucking idiot." I cursed myself now in shame, burying my head further in the pillow. Not only did I behave badly, but I'd compounded it by treating Adam like a pariah. "Oh, I'm going to hell for this."

Rachel and Adam still acted as though it was 'no big deal'. But I had always thought it was a big deal - a very big deal.

I just had no idea why.

5

Faith

I jumped when the phone on the bedside table rang, bringing me back to the present. Taking a big, deep breath, I answered. "About bloody time."

"Mum?"

"Scott. What's wrong? Why are you ringing so late?" I twisted my head around to glance at the illuminated digital clock-radio on the opposite bedside table.

"Mum, relax. It's not twelve yet."

Only just. I grimaced, noting it was 11:55 p.m.

"Were you expecting someone?" my son asked.

"Don't change the subject, buddy. What are you calling for?"

"I rang to tell you I'm not coming home tonight. I thought I might camp at Mick's place."

I heard muffled laughter in the background, making me feel suspicious.

"Well, this is a first, ringing to let me know."

"Yeah, well, I thought I'd do the right thing since you forced me to take your mobile out with me tonight," Scott replied, his tone coated in sarcasm.

"Sweetheart, if you hadn't dropped your phone in the toilet, you wouldn't have needed to take mine. Remember, you're paying for every phone call, too. What's so funny?"

"Nothing, why?"

"I can hear a lot of laughing in the background," I said, feeling mistrustful.

"The guys are hassling me cos I have to call home to Mummy."

The last was conveyed in a voice loud enough for his mates to hear. The laughter got louder.

"It's a common courtesy, Scott. You know I can't sleep properly until you get home, especially since you make such a racket when you get in. Then I'm awake forever," I patiently explained for the hundredth time. "Plus, I worry about you. Anyway," I added, sensing his eagerness to end the lecture. "I've got to go. I'm expecting an important call."

"Yeah?" His interest peaked. "At twelve o'clock at night? You got a boyfriend you haven't told me about, Mum?"

"I might have," I teased. Hearing his gasp, and not wanting to get his hopes up, I confessed, "No, actually it's just Rachel."

"Oh."

43

I heard the disappointment in his voice and smiled to myself. Scott was always urging me to go out on dates and had even tried to set me up on a blind date with his basketball coach. Losing interest, he was again in a hurry to end the call.

"Okay, see ya, Mum."

"Night, sweetheart."

I put the phone down and waited and waited. I was on the verge of nodding off when the telephone peeled. Startled into wakefulness I answered, my voice cranky. "Rachel, it's about time."

"Sorry mate, just got in. Steve isn't even asleep yet."

Which was really saying something on how fast she called, since Rachel swore her husband fell asleep the very second his head touched the pillow.

My heartbeat quickened in expectation. "What's the verdict?"

"Come on, you don't think I'm going to be that kind to you, do you?"

I groaned, fluffed up my pillows and made myself comfortable. I knew I was in for a long recital.

"First, I ..."

"Wait, wait, wait. Do I need to pour myself another scotch?" I asked.

"Another? What the hell, you ol' booze hag? No time for one more, and by the sounds, you've had one too many, ya 'one pot screamer'."

I laughed at how well she knew me. I was feeling drunk-sleepy.

"Okay, continue then."

"So, first I dropped your name into the conversation to gauge his reaction. He was cool. Interested, but cool. He'd brought along this blonde airhead to the folk's place. Like, he was expecting to spend the night with her ... in Mum and Pedro's house! What a prick. It's why we're so late. He didn't rock up until ten, and then Mum insisted on making him something to eat. You know how she panders to him."

I didn't like hearing about the woman he planned to sleep with, and felt a sharp stab of something ... jealousy, maybe? "Is this relevant to the story, Rach?"

She paused. "It is if you don't want me to hang up."

I ground my teeth. Rachel was an unfulfilled writer and dragged each story out to its maximum limit. "Sorry. Please continue at your leisure, Your Highness."

"Hmm, where was I ...? Oh right. Ads thinks he can just sneak in with blonde bimbo, expecting everyone to be in bed. But surprise, we waited for him to get home, much to Steve's disgust. But good to be honest, since the girls stayed the night, so we get a sleep-in tomorrow."

Rachel paused long enough to take a sip, no doubt from a coffee, before continuing.

"So, this chick, she had one of those flaky names, the kind drag queens always pick, Tiffany." Her name was said in derision. "She interrupts as soon as I bring up your name, and then dominates the conversation and Adam's attention for a good half hour. In the end, I made Steve ask her about her job, so you owe him one there. But get this, she's a masseuse - yeah right! Happy ending type, I bet."

I smiled widely to myself. I loved Rachel's bitchy comments. They were so in-tune with mine.

"Then, while Steve is talking to the strumpet, I approached Adam in a nonchalant manner and casually mentioned you'd asked after him the other day."

I held my breath. It was useless to even try to make Rachel get to the point, and in a masochistic sense, I was enjoying the story. Burrowing down under the blankets, I lay back to savour the experience.

"And what did he say?" I whispered the question, then held my breath.

My friend ignored me and went on undeterred with her story.

"Well … to say he was interested would be putting it mildly. It was quite comical, actually. He was standing on the back patio looking up at the stars, listening to my conversation in a half-hearted way, his mind wandering. You know how you can tell when someone isn't giving you their full attention? It's so annoying. So, I very quietly said, 'I saw Faith today, and she asked about you'."

Rachel paused here, allowing the impact of her words to be absorbed. It was a very subtle form of torture she had perfected over the years.

"Let me tell you, Faith, I wouldn't be at all surprised to see Adam in a neck-brace tomorrow. The way he snapped to attention, and twisted around at my words, he's sure to have whiplash."

My face split into a delighted grin at my companion's words. Biting down on my lips, I tried to gain control, but a bubble of laughter still escaped. "Go on, Rach. Don't make me suffer."

"He tried to appear aloof, but I was onto him. He was secretly delighted, could barely hide it. He asked what you'd wanted to know. So, I tortured him too. 'You know this and that,' I said. Then he asked about you, too. How you were doing since the divorce? How Scott was? Did you have a boyfriend? Did …"

"He didn't, did he?" I cut her off mid-sentence, sitting up abruptly in the bed, my voice squeaking in pleasurable surprise.

"He sure did, kiddo, in a casual, 'I'm just making conversation' kind of way. If you believe him? And I don't."

"It doesn't mean anything, Rachel." I had to bring Rachel and myself back down to earth. "He wants us to be friends again."

"Yeah sure, whatever you say." Even before 'the kiss', Rachel had always maintained Adam had the hots for me. For years it was a joke between us.

"So, I mentioned Rob was getting married and filled him in on all the gory details. I also told him about my great idea that he acts as your lover to boost your ego and make Rob think you've moved on, too."

Rachel paused in anticipation and I snuggled back down, punched my pillow into shape, and switched the phone to my other ear.

"It's still the plan, right?"

"Oh, definitely. What did he say?"

"I'm getting there, don't rush me."

I could hear Rachel's movements and could imagine her stretching out on the lounge room couch while her hubby was snoring in their bedroom. If she'd been in bed, she would no doubt be fluffing up her pillows too. I smiled at the similarities between us.

"He didn't like it, Faith. I have to be honest with you there. He said you should forget about that clown, and you could do better. I had to agree with him, but you already know what I think. Anyway, he reckons he owed you one and he would do it, no worries."

"Yeee," I squealed into the phone. "Wait ... What?" A

puzzled frown crumpled my brow. "What does he mean he owes me? For what?"

"I asked him. He claimed you knew."

"The hell I do. More like I owe him after the way I treated him." I sighed, "You were right Rachel, I blew 'the kiss' thing out of all proportion. I owe him an apology, big time." I chewed on my lip in distress.

"Yeah, I know Faith. Speaking of owing, I believe it's time you gave me an explanation. Why did you?"

I paused. "Yes, I do, too. Funny thing is, after making myself not think about it for years, I finally went over it in my head tonight; in painful, embarrassing detail." Then sarcastically I said, "I had plenty of time, since I waited hours for you to call me."

"But I did call. And with good news."

"True. Well, after going over it umpteen times and analysing it from every angle, I'm ready to confess at long last, why I blew it all up." I paused for a couple of seconds to build up my courage and then plunged on. "I was so turned on." There I said it. The words bubbled out unrestrained. "First the dance, and then the kiss. He was so deliciously sexy, and I was like this ... this desperate, sex-starved housewife. I wanted to devour him. My God, Rach, if the couple hadn't interrupted us, I would have had standing-up sex right there in your parents' front garden."

"Oh. My. Fucking. God. I knew it," Rachel crowed.

"But I was so eaten up with guilt. I was a married woman, Rachel, and the first time my husband goes out of town, I cheat. At least Adam had the excuse of being drunk. I was sober as a judge."

"Oh, Faith."

There was no censure or judgment in Rachel's voice,

just sorrow. Hot tears filled my eyes, and I blinked them back.

My voice broke when I said the next words, so faint my friend must have struggled to hear. "He was like my brother. I held him when he was an infant. I babysat him, fed him, put him to sleep."

"No, Faith." Rachel attempted to placate me. "He's not your brother. I can imagine how you must've been feeling, but it's okay. Babe, it's legal."

"No, it's not okay, Rachel. I felt like a filthy slut, taking advantage of a drunk kid."

I heard Rachel snort.

"Really? Because, I know my brother, Faith, and even at eighteen, and even drunk, there was no way you could have taken advantage of him. I've witnessed plenty, and I mean a shitload of girls try. If he didn't want what happened, believe me; there is no way it would've happened. Anyway, he instigated it. He put the moves on you, not the other way around."

I burst into tears, "Rachel ... God, I love you." I'd been carrying around the burden of guilt and censure for years. Half expecting her to shun me for my actions.

"I love you, too, babe. And you are not a filthy slut. You and Adam have always had this connection. It's never been a brother/sister thing. Okay, now you sound like a paedophile ... but honestly, you were always close friends. I was jealous at first, but then ..." Rachel paused. "You know what I think? What I truly believe?"

"No." My voice sounded small and hollow even to myself.

"I feel certain you and Adam are soulmates or something. Your souls must've recognized it subconsciously and were drawn to each other. You can't fight it, and neither can he."

Rachel's voice sounded smug. Like she'd figured it out a long time ago and only now was sharing this great wisdom.

"Do you think?" I felt cheered up. "You know, you could have something there." I gave a watery version of a smile.

"Unless of course you're like the brother and sister from Game of Thrones, and you are a filthy slut after all."

I laughed out loud. "Too soon, bitch. Too soon." A huge smile stretched my mouth. "You know, Rach, I'm so glad this has all come about. Not Rob getting married of course, but Adam and I making friends. I didn't realize how much I've missed him over the years."

"I'm glad, too. By the way, he's going to call you tomorrow for next weekend."

"Okay, now I'm feeling nervous," I wet my dry lips. "By the way, you were right today."

"The fuck?"

I heard a choking sound, like Rachel had taken a sip of her coffee and was coughing and banging her chest.

"Repeat that please, only louder. Much louder."

I threw my head back against the pillow and laughed. "Today when you said I didn't want to get back with Rob. I don't know why I ever wanted to now. But after examining my feelings, putting my marriage under the microscope, I realised we'd always been scratching at trying to make our relationship work. I sabotaged it at every turn. I was the one who wouldn't go to couple's therapy, and who refused to move away for his career. It was me who decided not to pursue treatment when I had trouble conceiving. I'm only now becoming aware of my subversive behaviour."

"Uh huh ... thank you. Say it." Rachel's voice was firm.

I giggled. "Say what?"

"You know," she snapped.

"Rachel, you were right. I do not want to get back with Rob."

"Yes."

"You're fist-pumping the air, right?" I asked rolling my eyes at her.

"Too right," she crowed. "I'm glad you finally, *finally*, admitted it."

"I'm sorry it took so long. I guess tonight has been a reawakening for me of sorts. Maybe I need to see a shrink?"

"Yeah, babe."

I heard a big yawn on the other end of the line and mirrored her yawn across town. I looked at the time.

Holy crap 1:25 a.m.

"I get the hint. Goodnight, Rach, and thank you so much."

Rachel grew serious. "Just don't hurt him again, Faith."

"I'll try not to."

"Goodnight, Faith."

"Oh Rachel, before you go." I grabbed her attention but then was hit by a wave of uncertainty at my question.

"Hmm?" I heard her sleepy response.

"The blonde girl tonight ...?" My question trailed off. Did I want to know?

"After your name was mentioned, he shuffled her

out." Rachel chuckled. "Tiffany was dropped off at her home by yours truly."

I beamed into the phone. "Thanks, Rach."

My best friend yawned loudly. "Go to sleep, Faith. Sweet dreams."

"Night."

I gently put down the phone.

Sweet dreams?

I had a feeling my dreams were going to include a beautiful man with a lopsided grin and wicked, wicked eyes.

6

Faith

Gazing at my reflection one last time, I scrunched my nose at the image before me. I'd taken great care with my appearance for this dinner, but like most women, I was never fully satisfied with my looks.

I'd allowed my friend, Jess, who owned the hairdresser's next to my own beauty salon, to give my hairstyle a make-over. First, she had cut my shoulder length hair shorter at the back, giving my locks a concave effect, tapering the overall length to swing freely a fraction above my shoulders. Then, she applied a handful of caramel coloured foils; the highlights adding warmth and depth to my otherwise mousy blonde tones.

My naturally wavy hair now had a sexy, tousled look. The effect was impressive, and I twirled around in front of the mirror in time to the classic Van Morrison song 'Brown-Eyed Girl', liking the way my hair swished around my face.

Did it make me look too young? It was times like this, I yearned to have a teenage daughter instead of a son. Someone to encourage or discourage this bold move. Rachel was great, but she was the 'damn the torpedoes, full steam ahead' type of person. She'd gone shopping with me and helped pick tonight's outfit.

"Leave it to me, Faith," she promised. "We'll knock their socks off. Let's go with the Bo-Ho style since it suits you, and now with your new do, you'll be stunning."

Rachel had excellent taste in clothes, and I was confident with the outfit she'd chosen. My dress was a multi-coloured loose fit shift in various shades of honey and gold with shoestring straps. The plainness of the light silky ensemble was offset by the many tiny brown and cream beads sewn around the low-cut bodice and bustline. Falling to just above my knee, it was casual but stylish.

Of course, Rachel had also insisted on sexy lingerie, winking at me in the shop and making loud comments about how I might get lucky, or how Adam would love the way my pussy would look in these knickers. I had to physically clamp my hand over her mouth and threaten her with death before she shut up. She gave me a raised brow look when we at last agreed on a coffee-coloured, sheer, flat lace strapless bra and matching boy-leg French knickers. It was the most decadent underwear I had ever worn.

I had my assistant at the salon give me an all over spray tan and waxing two days ago, and now my delicate gold anklet shimmered against my honey-bronzed skin. I slipped my feet into strappy brown summer sandals. The heels weren't too high and would bring me eye-level with Adam.

Thoughts of Adam made my heart do a little flip-flop. He had phoned on Saturday as promised, but not until late evening. I had spent the day jumping every time my phone rang, only to be disappointed by 9:00 p.m. when I still hadn't heard from him. When my mobile finally trilled later that night, I expected it to be Rachel again, for the hundredth time, and was shocked to hear his deep, sexy voice.

"Faith?" His tone sounded wary and unsure as if he was having second thoughts.

"Adam, I'm so glad you called. Actually, I'd almost given up hope you would call at all. Rachel told me she had spoken to you and you'd agreed to ..."

I cut short my rehearsed speech as a thought suddenly struck me. "You haven't changed your mind, have you?" I held my breath, my heart hammering wildly. I had been blabbering on and hadn't given him a chance to get a word in.

"No," he chuckled. "I haven't changed my mind, although I think ..." He broke off what he was about to say. "Never mind what I think ... If it's what you want. I feel like I owe you one."

I could feel a frown knit my brow at his words. "Rachel told me you'd said as much, but honestly Adam, it's me who owes you a very big apology. For slapping your face and saying those cruel things to you.

You must think I'm a complete bitch."

"Faith, I don't ..."

"No, Adam." I stopped him finishing his sentence. I had rehearsed my apology, and I wanted to finish it. "I overreacted to what was a harmless, if inappropriate, kiss." And other inappropriate, sexy, orgasmic things, I silently added. "And damaged our lifelong friendship. For that, I'm truly sorry. And to be quite honest, it wasn't like you twisted my arm or anything. I'm as much at fault as you."

There, I'd said it. After practicing all day, going over and over the words I'd mentally written down, they hadn't sounded quite as eloquent as they had in my mind. But at least I'd finally voiced my regret over the kiss.

"Faith, please don't. I owe you an apology, not the other way around. You were right, I should never have come onto you. You were married, and I was a young idiot. You had every right to be mad at me. You don't know how many times I've beaten myself up over what happened and wanted to turn back time to try to ... I don't know ... undo the damage, I guess. This is my opportunity to make it up to you if I can."

I could hear the torment in his voice. He sounded very upset and sincerely wanted to make it up to me, so after chatting for a few minutes, Adam arranged to pick me up the following weekend.

When I'd put down the phone, it was as though a great weight had been lifted from my shoulders. I had religiously carried around this crucifix of guilt on my back for the past eleven years, and only now realized just how burdensome it had been. I felt light, happy, and even excited about what had been, up to now, a very lonely future.

Adding dangling gold and topaz earrings and a matching necklace, I gave my reflection one last glance. Swiping a cinnamon lip gloss over my lips, I whirled away from the bathroom mirror at the sound of a car pulling into the drive.

Peeking out from between the vertical blinds, I saw Adam climbing out of an immaculate charcoal-grey, four-wheel-drive vehicle. Long legs encased in slim-line black trousers strained over a tight butt as he closed the car door but leaned in through the window to throw his sunglasses onto the dashboard.

My, my, if it were possible, he really had improved with age.

I dashed down the hallway to the front door, pausing before it to calm my racing heart.

"Hi," I sighed in sheer pleasure when I swung it wide, my eyes drinking in the beauty of the man before me. His crooked grin made an appearance, his wicked eyes dancing before he stepped in the doorway and scooped me up into a tight bear hug.

"Fate."

Just the one word. His simple, childish, pet name for me. But it made me want to cry. It made me want to shout with joy. I had to swallow the lump in my throat and blink away the silly moisture crowding my eyes.

It may have been from almost being crushed to death in his embrace, but I didn't mind. Adam was back. My Adam was back.

I hugged him right back, my feet leaving the floor as he lifted me up and into his arms. It felt so right to be like this, wrapped in his warmth.

Gradually, he let me go, holding me at arm's length

to look at me. Really look at me. And I was looking at him, too. Although I'd seen him only over a week ago, the awkwardness of the meeting had made it too uncomfortable to study him openly. Now I did, and I liked what I saw.

He'd aged. Gone was the smooth, boyish skin of youth, replaced with a slight stubble jaw. The kind of jaw made for nibbling, for lips to scrape across the sandpapery texture in an exploratory journey from chin to ear.

Wicked cobalt eyes, bracketed by sun-bronzed laugh lines fanning out from their lash-rimmed allurement, crinkled when he smiled. His nose, just this side of too big, suited him.

But his mouth ... Oh God, his gorgeous, lopsided mouth. With firm, masculine lips, it was too wide, and was the only thing saving him from being perfect. But how I loved it. Those strong white teeth combined with his sexy, wolfish smiles, which dipped down on one side of his face had always captivated me. I'd place odds many women had fantasized about that imperfect mouth. And now, I could openly admit I was one of them.

His short hair was still a deep, rich chocolate. Mussed as usual. Adam had a habit of raking his fingers through his hair repeatedly. On anyone else, it would be a bad hair day, every day. On him, it was sexily suggestive. My fingers itched to smooth it back in place the way I had done on so many occasions in the past. Instead, I curled them into a fist at my side.

My scrutiny moved down his body. Wide shoulders, narrow waist, lean hips and long legs, my eyes made an inventory of all his assets. He wore a deep burgundy, long-sleeved shirt, the sleeves rolled to below his elbows. The colour emphasised his dark, smouldering looks. He reeked of sensuality. Something I definitely hadn't noticed years ago.

"Stunning."

Adam's one word of approval of the effort I'd taken with my appearance mirrored my own thoughts. It was rewarding, and I beamed.

"I could say the same."

After I closed the front door, the previously spacious entry felt intimate and close. We both stood and stared at each other.

"Would ... would you like to come in and have a drink before we go?" Swallowing nervously, I stepped aside to allow him further access into my home.

It was the same house he'd been to before. After the divorce, I'd refinanced and put the house into my name. We had the house built only months after Scott had been born, and I had put too much time and effort into the decorating to want to move away. My beautician business and the school was within walking distance, so it didn't seem logical to leave. Plus, the house held a lot of happy memories for Scott and me.

"What would you like to drink? Scott's gone to pick up his girlfriend, Michelle, so he shouldn't be too long." I led the way down the hallway to the open-plan kitchen/family room. "I've got beer or white wine, or scotch, and if we're really lucky, maybe some Jacks."

"A beer would go down well."

He followed me into the kitchen and propped himself up against the benchtop. The setting sun turned the kitchen into a fiery blaze of orange, slanting in through the huge sliding glass doors which led onto a brick-paved patio in the back garden. On very hot days the room became a furnace. I'd taken to barbecuing at these times, usually after the sun had disappeared.

Handing him an icy cold beer and pouring a wine for myself, I nodded towards the back door. "Shall we sit outside? It's unbearable in here at this time of the day."

"Sure."

After we were seated on the comfortable cane setting, 'Dude', my large orange tabby tom cat, ambled up to Adam, yowling for attention.

"Yours, I presume?"

"Yes. 'Dude'."

Adam chuckled as the aptly named creature rubbed himself against his legs.

"I wish it were true, but to be honest, it's more like I'm his. He is one hundred percent the boss and I believe he's come to pass judgment on you. He mysteriously appears whenever someone new is over, to inspect and give either his approval or disapproval."

I had barely finished the sentence when with one mighty leap, 'Dude' had launched himself onto Adam's lap. Startled, he snapped back into the chair.

I burst out laughing. "Oh, he approves of you all right."

Adam was busy scratching the tiger-like feline behind his left ear, while the cat gave a loud purr. "I'd hate to see what he does when he disapproves."

"Something nasty to be sure," I warned. "He can either swish his tail into your food or knock your drink off the table with one quick swipe. Or sometimes, he might cough up a hairball onto your shoe."

We both laughed at the antics of my wicked feline as I went on to recite some more of his nasty habits. When

Scott and Michelle found us, we were laughing so hard, I had tears streaming from my eyes.

"Hey, Adam." Scott bounded across the patio.

Adam got to his feet, dislodging a now grouchy feline, and stared at a near fully-grown Scott before clasping hands in a hand-wrestling hold. He pulled him into his embrace, clapping him on the back.

"Scott, mate. I can't believe you're all grown up. Jeez, look how tall he is?" His gaze met and held mine. Like me, he was probably remembering a younger version of himself playing with a much smaller Scott.

Releasing Scott, he shook his head in wonder. "You're the image of your old man."

I took in the situation, noting Scott's silly grin, which was no doubt identical to the one I wore. I was so proud of my wonderful son. Seeing their fondness for each other made me feel bad. Another victim of the forced separation I'd incited all these years. They could have been such close friends, and Adam would have been a great mentor for Scott.

After introducing Michelle, who couldn't keep her eyes off Adam, the two men became absorbed in a conversation about school, sport, and of course cars, now that Scott had acquired his driver's license.

After touching up my lip-gloss and scrunching my hair one last time, I called out from the front door. "Come on, guys, we'd better get going or else we'll be late."

7

Faith

We decided to go to the restaurant in Adam's car. The drive normally didn't take long, but today it seemed to drag. I was conscious of Adam sitting only inches away, separated by the console between the bucket seats. My gaze kept wandering to his long-fingered hands adeptly changing gear, the muscles in his thighs bulging as he pushed the clutch in and out.

I wriggled more comfortably into the black leather seat admiring the dashboard, which resembled the cockpit of a jet rather than a car. Accents of black, charcoal, and silver framed a large centrally located touch screen, giving the vehicle a technical touch to the luxury, while the many coloured lights proclaimed its functionality.

The conversation inside the vehicle revolved around questions asked and answered by Adam regarding his car. Scott was new to driving and was saving his money to buy himself a small four-wheel-drive, hence the interrogation. I took the opportunity of being excluded to mentally prepare myself for the evening ahead.

Breathing out deeply to release some of my nervous tension, I threw a wobbly smile at Adam. I had plenty of reasons to be nervous meeting Shania, a woman whom I heard was near to perfection. It made it so damn difficult to find anything interesting regarding myself to feel good about. My only few consolations were that Scott was loyal in the extreme, I had Adam at my side, and I knew I looked good. Well, as good as I was going to get.

When we pulled into the parking lot of the trendy tavern Rob had chosen to dine in, Scott and Michelle scrambled from the vehicle and raced over to introduce Michelle to the couple waiting near the front door who had conveniently arrived moments before. Taking advantage of their preoccupation, I studied them.

I cringed when I caught sight of Rob's fiancée - the complete opposite of me. She looked to be in her mid-twenties, small and petite, yet curvy and sexy looking at the same time. Her white-blonde hair was caught up into a sophisticated clasp at the back of her head, making it difficult to determine its length. She wore a skin-tight white dress made from some stretchy fabric which moulded to her slim body, clinging onto and highlighting large breasts, and was bordering on indecent. The short mini length showing the perfection of slender legs, which looked twice as long in the three-inch heels.

Oh, that's fucking great!

"Are you okay, Faith?" Adam inquired gently.

He must have noticed my stricken expression I was trying hard to disguise. He put a warm, reassuring hand over both of mine, which were clenched in my lap.

"Oh, just dandy." My words came out in a sarcastic snap. "Sorry. I expected the worst, but I didn't expect her to be even worse than the worst." I gave a shaky little laugh. "If that makes sense."

"It makes perfect Faith-sense," he replied and laughed.

He gave me a hard stare, probably making sure I was all right, before he got out of the car and came around to my side. I was already standing on the pavement when he reached me, so after locking the door, he folded my hand in his, intimately twining our fingers together.

"Come on, let's face the music."

As we approached, both couples stopped chatting and turned in unison toward us. I noticed Shania's eyes briefly skim over me to settle on Adam. She actually licked her lips.

Rob frowned in recognition of Adam. I wasn't sure if he noticed the interest from his girlfriend or not, but I smiled to myself - the evening might be fun after all.

Ignoring Adam altogether, Rob proceeded to introduce me to his betrothed. Shania tore her gaze from Adam and offered her hand, along with a brilliant smile.

"Hi Faith, I've looked forward to meeting you."

Surprised by her friendly greeting, I smiled in

return, but fought back irritation when the other woman's focus quickly moved back onto Adam.

"This is Adam Warner. A close friend of mine." Reluctantly I made the introduction.

Adam held his hand out to the smaller woman, his large fingers almost swallowing up her delicate one. Only the pale polish on her nails peeked out.

"I think we may have met before. You seem very familiar." Shania flashed a flirty smile at Adam.

I rolled my eyes at the obvious pick up line. Unfortunately, Rob caught the look. His pale blue eyes narrowed on me in a warning glare. I shrugged my shoulders.

"I'm sure I wouldn't forget you if we had met before Shanna," Adam remarked politely.

Shania preened.

"It's Shania," Rob corrected, a frown on his face.

Looking across at Robert, Adam nodded. "Newman."

"Warner."

No love lost there. My ex-husband had always resented the amount of time I'd spent with Adam. Even when Adam was still riding around on his push-bike, Rob had complained, 'Doesn't that kid have a home to go to?'

Because of the obvious friction between them, I'd taken great pains to keep Adam out of Robert's way. It wasn't too difficult since Rob was rarely at home before dark, and the weekends found him working in his office or at the squash courts, his other love. It looked as though nothing had changed.

We entered through large wooden doors into a delightful beer garden. Steel-framed tables with wood tops were scattered around the brick-paved area. Large terracotta tubs and planters filled with palms and dracaenas provided greenery, while hanging baskets hung from the pergola roof, overflowing with cascading petunias.

Stepping inside, I allowed my eyes to adjust to the darkness within. Tasteful tables and chairs with crisp white linen cloths and cutlery shining under the strategically placed down lights, greeted us. Muted music piped through ceiling speakers dotted around the room, made for a classy establishment. As with the beer garden, over-sized potted palms and indoor plants discreetly sat dividing diners from each other.

We made our way into the bar and ordered drinks before the meal. I climbed onto the black leather barstool and Adam slipped his arm around my waist, staking a proprietorial claim. I was secretly thrilled to be getting not only his attention, but Rob's attention as well, even if it was a scowl.

Robert flicked his thinning sandy hair out of his eyes. His navy-blue trousers and light blue and white striped shirt were casual-dressy but lacked the stylish sexiness of Adam. He wore a thick gold chain, and I noticed a man's gold engagement ring gracing his finger, a diamond twinkling on the band.

My eyes quickly flicked to Shania's rock on her ring finger. It was a white-gold band with an over-size princess cut diamond. A circle of smaller diamonds surrounded it. It looked to be worth a small fortune. Pretentious, as I'd expected. I inwardly smirked.

The women in the bar, including present company, kept throwing me envious glances. No doubt because of Adam.

Good God, he seemed to affect all females within a

five-metre radius.

When I looked up at him to see if he noticed, Adam smiled down and pushed a strand of hair off my forehead with one finger. I knew it was all a show for Rob's benefit, but it didn't mean I couldn't enjoy it as my stomach did a little dance at the gesture.

I draped my arm around his waist and rubbed my hand up and down his back as he stood at the bar, hoping he wouldn't mind my daring.

He held himself very still, and then I felt it. Almost an electrical charge.

Oh, he liked it all right.

Adam arched his back in what I assumed to be enjoyment and leaned into me. In another moment I expected him to start purring aloud like 'Dude'.

Instead, he did the human equivalent. Turning to me, his mouth curved upward into a slow, stunning smile; the one I'd secretly named his sex-on-steroids grin, which liquefied my bones, and nuzzled his face into my neck. He inhaled deeply, breathing in my fragrance.

"Do you think this will fool them?" he whispered.

"Uh, huh."

It was the only thing I could think of to say. Any intelligent comment was out of the question. Especially when I felt his lips softly grazing against my throat.

"I... OH!"

He licked me. He actually licked me.

I clutched the edge of the bar with one hand and hung onto his shoulder for dear life. I had read in romance books about getting weak at the knees. It was fiction of course, but in that moment, if I were required to stand or walk, I would have fallen to the ground in a quivering mess.

Adam turned and ordered our drinks from the barman who now stood in front of us, a knowing smirk on his lips as he observed our show. I wasn't even aware of his approach and cringed inwardly. If Adam hadn't been alert, and turned away from me, I would have thrown back my head to give him easier access to my throat and more.

I turned glazed eyes onto Adam. He smiled, unrepentant, and motioned with his eyes to the other side of me. When I turned to look, I met four sets of eyes, all with varying degrees of reaction.

Rob wore an irritated frown of censure. Shania's gaze narrowed in envy. Michelle was wide-eyed in surprise, and Scott ... Well if eyes could give a thumbs up, his would be doing just that.

I felt the heat rise into my face and was grateful when Adam took the lead.

"Well, since we all have our drinks, shall we grab a table?"

Robert had booked a large round table furthest from the dance floor and the DJ who was busy setting up his equipment. By unconscious agreement, Scott and Michelle were strategically placed between me and Rob. With the boy/girl configuration, it left Shania sitting next to Adam, a situation I found displeasing. Robert did as well, his attempt to swap places having no effect on his girlfriend. She was having none of it.

There was an exchange of pleasantries and information before studying the menu and ordering our meals from the hovering waiter.

No sooner had the waiter left when Rob began boasting how clever Shania was. A fellow accountant in his firm, they were considering promoting her since she brought in so much business.

"Doesn't your old man own the business?" Scott asked his future stepmother.

My foot gave his, a soft kick under the table, and I had to bite my lip in amusement at Scott's question. It made everyone seated aware that with this marriage, Robert was putting his 'dick in the till'.

His dad threw him an annoyed frown. "She still had to get a degree and her CPA," he reminded.

"What's that, Mr. Newman?" Michelle's little voice was barely heard at the table. I glanced at her, noting her long brown hair had been straightened with an iron and hung on either side of her pretty face in a silky curtain. Her blue eyes were curious as she looked between Rob and Shania.

Shania answered for Robert.

"It's a Certified Practicing Accountant, Michelle. To become a CPA, a candidate must hold a degree or a postgraduate award which is recognised by CPA Australia. You must be able to demonstrate competence in the required knowledge area and successfully complete the CPA program, which takes six years. I wish I'd done something which didn't require so much education sometimes, like you Faith," Shania stated with a petulant sigh. "I leave work so brain-dead at times, I just want to flop on the lounge in front of the TV and veg out."

And there it was. Maybe I was being paranoid, but I felt the subtle dig, comparing our choice in professions and education level, and could only nod in simmering agreement.

"Well, someone has to make you women look even

more awesome," Adam stated to the table. "What would you do without hairdressers, manicurists and beauticians?"

Adam wrapped his fingers around my hand, lifting it to his lips and kissing the back. He looked into my eyes with a twinkle. "Just look how gorgeous Faith looks tonight. Am I right?"

Scott hooted, "Mum, you look awesome. It's why my mates call you a MILF."

"Scott!" I blushed but smiled at my two loyal protectors sitting either side of me. Of course, I was familiar with the acronym 'mother I'd like to fuck', made popular by the entertainment industry, but I never imagined my son's friends viewed me in such a way. It made me somewhat uncomfortable.

"Hear, hear." Adam grinned at me.

Shania didn't look too happy at those words, but she was a fighter and came back with a low blow.

"Speaking of mothers, we have some news." She turned and smiled at Rob. His face held a startled expression.

"We're expecting a baby at the end of the year," she happily announced.

My eyes flew to Scott. He seemed as surprised as I did. We both looked askance at my ex-husband.

He put his arm around his fiancée's shoulders, an awkward look flashing across his features.

"This isn't exactly how I wanted to tell you, but it's true. Shania is eight weeks pregnant."

Now the news was out, his expression looked proud.

My fingers tightened on Adam's. I felt like I'd been sucker punched. I had tried to have more children, but after miscarriage after miscarriage, I gave up in the end. It had always been a bone of contention between us. Robert had wanted more children and urged me to try in-vitro-fertilization, but I had refused, our relationship was struggling.

I felt Adam squeeze my hand as I plastered a false smile on my face and forced words out.

"Well, I guess celebrations are in order. Congratulations."

At least it explains the surprise wedding.

I couldn't stop the bitchy thought from entering my head, and I bit my lip before I said something I might regret. I badly needed a drink.

Reaching for my glass, I lifted it up. "All the best, you two. For the baby and the upcoming nuptials."

Everyone raised their glasses in a toast. I sculled my wine like it was cordial.

I felt Adam's eyes burning into me, but I didn't look at him. I didn't want him to feel sorry for me. Instead, he flagged a passing waiter and ordered another bottle of wine for me.

"Let's get fucking smashed," he whispered in my ear.

I grinned at him.

"Oh my God, you aren't even showing," Michelle squealed in admiration.

Shania stood up and showed off her flat belly in the tight white dress, while Rob possessively put a hand over her tummy.

"She's one of those lucky ones who stay thin, no matter what," my ex-husband haughtily beamed.

So was I, I thought but kept my mouth shut and drank more wine while still processing the information. I looked at Scott to gauge his reaction, he seemed a bit put out by it all.

Ordinarily, you couldn't expect a seventeen-year-old teenage boy to care one way or another if he has a little brother or sister. But the fact this was presented to us so soon after the wedding announcement must have thrown him off balance. It sure had thrown me off.

While Michelle asked baby questions, I excused myself to go to the bathroom. I felt Robert's and Scott's eyes on me as I got up. Adam stood up as well.

"I have to make a quick call," he declared, and walked with me in the direction of the toilets. "Are you okay?"

He placed a hand gently on my back.

I looked up at him, thankful of his concern, but also not wanting to make a fuss about it

"Right at this moment, I only want to focus on getting through the night Ads. There'll be plenty of time later to take in all the baby news and how it's going to affect Scott and I."

He nodded, a cheeky smile twisting his lips and a devilish sparkle in his eyes.

"What?" I asked.

He stopped before the doorway to the bathroom and pulled me to face him. He bent his head slightly and looking deep into my eyes, made a solemn promise. "If you ever want to make a baby, Faith, I'm your man." He winked suggestively and made a small thrusting motion with his hips.

I laughed. He always knew how to make me snap out of my funk. Biting my lip, I replied with a smile, "I'll keep it in mind, stud."

The dinner progressed as awkwardly as I expected. Yet I enjoyed it more than I thought I would, thanks to Adam. He was very attentive to me and should have won an Oscar for his performance.

With his arm draped behind my chair, his fingers caressed my shoulder, fiddling with the thin strap of my dress, or sliding down and stroking a bare arm or my back when I leaned forward.

Occasionally, he would lean over to me, burying his face into my neck to whisper something totally mundane like, 'I think these chips are great.' Or, 'pass the salt.'

But everyone else thought he was saying naughty things as I would look guiltily around the table and blush or giggle at the sexy tone he put on.

And just when I thought I'd gotten control of my flushing, his husky voice whispered, "I really want to lick you again."

I couldn't help my reaction. I pulled back with a shocked expression and looked at his hungry eyes, my own questioning whether it was an act or not.

Adam made sure my wine was topped up when getting low and pulled me into the conversation whenever Shania tried to engage him and leave me out.

At one stage when Robert's partner asked Adam if he was enjoying his meal he replied, "Mmm hmm, delicious. Taste this steak, babe."

He turned towards me with a piece of beef on his fork, covered with peppered sauce, a twinkle in his eye.

I opened my mouth dutifully, and he fed me the food.

"Mmm yum."

I nodded while chewing the mouthful before swallowing. Adam seductively wiped a spot of sauce from my lips with his finger and put it into his own mouth.

"Oh, yeah. So delicious." He winked at me.

I had to bite my lip at his antics. I glanced at Rob who for some reason was seething. I smiled at him, shrugging my shoulders.

When the meals were complete, the DJ started playing music and a few people populated the dance floor. We all watched in silence before Adam's phone rang and he left to take the call outside, away from the noise.

Robert leaned across the table his thin face screwed up into lines of displeasure. "Faith, you are making a fool of yourself."

I looked embarrassed at Scott. He and Michelle were preoccupied in a conversation of their own and missed my ex-husband's snarled words.

"I don't think so."

"You don't?" He looked at Shania. "Don't you think she's acting like some desperate housewife, trying to get me jealous?"

Shania had a contrite expression on her face and nodded.

I was fuming. "Well, you have nothing to worry about, unless of course you are feeling jealous?"

"I'm not the jealous one." He looked outraged at the suggestion. "You're only embarrassing yourself and your son. And stop drinking so much. You're drunk."

I glanced at Scott again. We now had his and Michelle's attention. My son had a worried look on his face.

I squared my shoulders. I was having a good time and refused to be brought down by these two losers.

"You two should be over the moon, you're getting married and having a baby. You should feel glad I've moved on and I'm happy. Adam has been in my life forever, and how we decide to conduct our relationship is our business and no one else's. Especially not yours, Rob."

Adam arrived back at our table at that opportune time. I was unsure if he picked up any of what I had said, but his presence seemed to shut the other couple up.

"They're playing our song," he announced. Wrapping his large hand over my smaller one, Adam hauled me up and wound his way through the tables onto the dance floor.

I was fuming after my conversation with Rob and Shania and was more than happy to have a break from them. Adam folded me into his arms and held me tightly, his mouth to my ear.

"It's such a turn on when you tell that selfish bastard off."

"I can't believe he accused me of embarrassing myself," I said indignantly. "He ... who has knocked up a girl seventeen years younger than him. She's young enough to be his daughter."

"Who cares, Faith? Forget about him. He didn't make you happy. He never will."

Adam's words were so simple, yet so true. I looked up at him and suddenly realised the things I'd voiced in the heat of the moment to Rob were true. I have moved on, and I am happy.

Someone bumped into us and I was brought back to reality. The postage stamp sized dance floor was now crowded with couples, swaying to the slow music. Adam scooped me even closer and crooned into my ear the words to the eighties classic, Careless Whisper.

My eyes grew wide as a subconscious memory surfaced. I felt light-headed and breathless as I realized, it was, in fact, 'our' song – Careless Whisper by George Michael. The very same song we had danced to at Adam's eighteenth birthday party so many years ago.

8

Adam

Faith pulled back in my arms and looked at my face. A stunned expression crossed her features. I knew she remembered.

"You know?" she asked, as we moved in unison on the crowded dance floor.

I smiled gently into her eyes, and they softened to a rich gold as she became aware I, too, was thinking back to the night so many years before. What a weird coincidence.

Or ... maybe, there were no coincidences in life, and this was meant to happen.

The crazy notion took root in my mind and remained

there, convincing me it was fate. Ah, Fate. No wonder it had always been my pet name for her.

I badly wanted to kiss her, and I couldn't seem to stop myself from carrying out the act once the thought flicked through my mind. I was always weak when I was around her and acting like the doting boyfriend all night had taken its toll on my self-control.

Who am I kidding? I wasn't acting at all.

Sliding both arms around her waist, I pulled her body into mine. At the first touch of my lips, hers were cool and wary, but before she could pull back, I increased the pressure, my kiss becoming possessive.

I heard her small gasp of surprise before she cautiously gave in to me. It was all the invitation I needed. Satisfaction coursed through me, and I meshed my lips to hers in slow measured degrees until they were joined. Then sliding my arms up to the back of her head and cupping it between both of my hands, I pressed her harder against my mouth.

My tongue slipped between her lips, twining around her own as I kissed her thoroughly. The sweetness of the dessert wine she had with her meal, combined with her own honeyed taste, almost sent me over the edge.

Although the music still played in a corner of my conscious mind, and I had a vague impression of other dancers who looked on entertained, I was so caught up in the moment, I couldn't have pulled back even if I'd wanted to. A part of me was aware we stood in the middle of the floor. The other part, the 'I couldn't give a fuck part', shut out everything but Faith.

This made up for all those years away from her. The years when she refused to see me, subconsciously scared of this. This wild joining of old friends; of lovers reacquainting in the way it never was but should have been.

She returned my kiss with a burning hunger. Then slipping her arms around my back, hands sliding down to my butt, she pulled my hips against hers as we moved to the music in a hypnotic, sexy sway.

Uh Oh. I felt myself harden in arousal against her hips. Reluctantly, and with a superhuman effort, I lifted my head abruptly and looked at Faith. Her golden gaze clouded with confusion. She looked drugged and dazed with her own stimulation. Her lips were soft, swollen, and parted in surprise. I wanted to continue kissing her, inhale her and draw her back down into my lungs like the sweet drug she was to me. And as much as I wanted to say 'fuck off' to everyone around me, lower her to the ground and make love; I came to my senses.

I knew exactly when Faith came to hers.

Her eyes filled with horror at what had just happened, and her face flamed as she looked around at the amused expressions of the surrounding people. The full force of what we had just done hit home.

I spied Scott and Michelle in a dark corner on the edge of the dance floor. Faith's son gave me a 'rock n roll' hand gesture, his tongue sticking out crudely in approval.

Oh shit, I hope Faith didn't see him.

Still looking somewhat stunned at the public spectacle she had been a party to, I wasted no time to wrap an arm over her shoulder and turn her around to head back to the table before she had time to react; or overreact.

On second thoughts ... After spotting Rob and Shania, both waiting eagerly, no doubt to berate Faith about her conduct, I maneuvered her zombie-like toward the front door for a bit of fresh air.

Although I had only caught the tail end of Faith's words to her ex-husband and his fiancée, I'd put two and two together to work out they'd made negative comments about Faith and myself - accusing her of embarrassing herself.

But she had bit back, tiger that she was. I was proud of her. I just hoped my lack of control hadn't made the situation worse for her, or she didn't go all prim and proper on me again.

I pulled her out through the beer garden and into the near empty parking lot. Once outside she turned to me.

"What the hell did we just do, Ads?" Not waiting for a reply, she continued, "We just fucking made out on the dance floor, that's what. In front of everyone. Oh, God ..." She dropped her head in her hands. "In front of Scott and Michelle. And worse ... in front of Rob and Shania. I'm never going to hear the end of this."

"I know." I looked down at her, in mock sadness, trying to decipher her mood. "How fucking awesome are we?" I proclaimed, laughing at her outraged look.

She bit her lip and beamed at me.

"Pretty bloody awesome."

There's my girl.

I picked her up and spun her around, delighted at her words. "Mrs. Newman, you are so naughty."

The burly bouncer on the door snickered and went to stand inside the door and give us some privacy.

"We made a spectacle like a couple of horny teenagers," she reprimanded.

I stopped spinning but still held her. "Don't worry about Scott. He's cool with it."

"What? What do you mean? How do you know?"

"He pulled me aside earlier in the evening when we went to the bar. He more or less implied if I wanted to become your boyfriend, that was 'sweet', to use his words."

Faith looked shocked for about two seconds. "Oh, the little rat-bag." She grinned.

"Faith?"

It was Robert.

Her smile vanished. He and Shania stood in the doorway. She had her handbag slung over her shoulder.

I put Faith down and we turned toward the couple.

"We're leaving. I suggest you do the same and either sober up or get a room for God's sake," he complained, clearly put out by our display.

I saw Faith shrug in dismissal. "We might just do that," she replied with her newfound smart-ass attitude.

I bit back a smile. I wanted to high-five her, but stood behind, touching her arm in support instead.

I glanced at my watch. It was 9:45 p.m. Before they could say any mean comments to burst Faith's bubble of happiness and confidence, I navigated the conversation.

"You must be tired, being pregnant and all. Thanks for a great night." I put my hand out to Rob, and he automatically shook it. "Great to catch up with you again, Newman." I turned to his girlfriend, offering my hand to her as well. "Nice to meet you Shania. Good luck with the wedding and baby."

I put an arm around Faith's waist and propelled her toward the entrance door.

The bouncer, watching the exchange, held the door

open for us.

"All the best, you two," Faith called out, raising a hand in farewell as I dragged her back into the tavern.

"What was that all about?" Faith asked me.

"I didn't want to talk to them, and neither did you I'm guessing, so ... what more was there to say, except goodbye?"

Faith giggled. "Good call."

I loved tipsy Faith.

We both went back to join Scott and Michelle at the table. After another wine for her and just Coke for me since I was driving, we stayed for another hour.

I'd never seen Faith happier. Dancing and even singing a karaoke song with me - ruining it, if truth be told, she could not hold a tune - before I drove her home.

When we arrived at Faith's house, Scott and Michelle left to spend the night at her place. Before he left, he hugged his mum and gave her a kiss.

"You kids behave now," he teased, winking to me over the top of her head.

"I saw that, Scott Newman," she yelled out at him as he climbed into his car.

He threw an outrageous laugh our way, before gunning it down the road.

After Scott left, we stood awkwardly together on the front porch. She made no attempt to open the door, and we stood in silence for so long, the sensor light on her porch switched off. Plunged into darkness, she released an uneasy laugh and waved her arm around until the light came on again.

I felt Faith needed the minutes to ponder our situation. I knew she was debating whether to invite me in or not. Because if she did, we both knew it would only end in one way.

The wait was unbearable, and just when I had decided not to push the relationship and leave, she turned to me looking up into my face.

"Thank you so much, Adam. I had a wonderful night. You have been such a good friend to me. I don't deserve you."

There was hesitation laced through her words, gazing downward again as she twisted her door-key in her hands in a nervous gesture.

Here we go. After all the progress I'd thought we made tonight, I was demoted back to her good friend. She simply couldn't get past the friend/brother thing.

I sighed, looking up at the clear night sky, and combing my fingers through my hair in frustration, before snapping my head back, astonished at her shy words.

"I realise it's late but ... would you like to come in for coffee?"

9

Adam

I turned sharply to her. A guarded look was etched on her face. But before she could change her mind, I took the house-key from her fidgeting fingers and opened the door.

"I'm hanging for a coffee."

She gave a shaky laugh, and left with no option, she stepped into the entrance hall.

Once inside, she boiled the kettle.

"The evening went well. It was far more entertaining than I had imagined." Faith pulled out two mugs from the overhead cupboard.

"Agreed. I think we managed to entertain everyone

there."

Faith snickered at my words. "The look on Robert's face ..."

"I know. I've seen lemons less sour," I chuckled. "Who knew he would be so uptight?"

Faith spooned instant coffee into the cup before her, pausing with a spoonful of granules hovering over the second one as a thought occurred. "I bet he calls me tomorrow to give me a serve."

"For sure."

Crossing the room, I opened the fridge and pulled the bottle of milk out, handing it to Faith. After pouring the hot water and adding milk, we carried our mugs to the family room.

It wasn't a large room, but the cream tiles gave the area an airy quality, making it appear bigger than it actually was; as an architect, it was something I appreciated. A large, fat, oatmeal coloured sofa dominated the space, while marri-wood coffee and side tables housed various tasteful ornaments. Overall, the room was elegant while remaining homey. It had been renovated since my time and I approved of the changes.

She placed the cups onto leather coasters and switched on a large table lamp, which cast an intimate glow into the room.

"It's more comfortable here," she said and slipped off her sandals.

I watched her wriggle her bronze-polished toes into the beige plush pile carpet.

"Wow, that's some TV." I admired the large, sixty-inch flat screen television the couch faced.

"I know," Faith rolled her eyes. "Scott insisted we needed a 'smart' TV. You know men and their obsession with everything electronic." She gave an indulgent chuckle.

I made myself comfortable at the other end of the sofa, turning to face her and bent a knee to rest on the cushion between us, my arm extended out along the back. She curled her legs up behind her, and facing me as well, she mimicked my arm resting on the back of the sofa, so our fingers were only a few inches apart.

I wondered if Faith had invited me in because she didn't want to be alone. Well, if all she wanted was a good friend, that criteria had exceeded its use-by-date a long time ago. I wanted more. Much more. And if Faith was honest, so did she.

But, if baby-steps was what I needed to do to make her realize the truth, well then, a good friend I would be. A very, very good friend. One with benefits.

We drank our coffee and reminisced about good times, laughing often. I closed the space between our hands and played with her fingers as we talked.

My much larger digits stroked hers and caressed the inside of her wrist, threading with hers while applying subtle pressure to pull her closer to my side of the couch until we sat inches apart facing each other.

I played an understated game of seduction, toying with her hair and pushing it behind her ear, while allowing my touch to linger longer than necessary. Flicking her dangly earrings, I touched her collar to stop their sway, caressing her skin in the process.

Faith was fully aware of what I was doing. She was allowing it. But how far I could take the touching at this stage was another matter. I didn't mind the slow progress too much, because from my vantage point, I had a nice view of her cleavage. Reaching a hand over, I touched the beads on the top of her dress, admiring the fine work, my fingertips lightly grazed the mounds of her breasts. She caught her breath but didn't move away. It encouraged me to continue.

I didn't want the evening to end, and was confident Faith felt the same but all too soon we'd finished our second cup of coffee. I glanced at my watch. 1:00 am - time to make a move one way or another.

"Can I use the bathroom?" I stood up and made my way down the hall.

When I returned Faith was standing at the small end of the breakfast bar, her back to me. She was folding the tea towel she'd used to dry the coffee cups.

"It's late. I guess I'd better be going," I said, coming up behind her.

Faith turned to face me our bodies close.

"Or ..." I ran my finger under the strap of her dress sliding it off her shoulder. "I could stay the night." My voice was huskier than intended, passion making my words thick.

Lifting my gaze from her arm, I searched her eyes. The golden orbs, normally a light topaz, had deepened to a warm, dark honey, desire evident in their depths. She reached out a hand and laid it gently against my chest. I was sure she could feel the hammering of my heartbeat against her palm. With her other hand, she traced tentative fingertips across my lips in a seductive gesture. My muscles tightened in response, and I remained statue-still as her tongue came out to wet her own dry lips.

A hoarse groan was torn from me, and suddenly, no longer able to resist, I pulled her into my arms and my lips found hers. I wanted to take it slow, but my mouth had other ideas and crushed hers in ravenous greed. I devoured her with burning, unrestrained kisses, hauling her body up to sit on the edge of the counter. Faith wrapped her legs around my hips as I pressed her ever closer.

She returned the fire with a longing of her own. Her hands wrapped around me, fingers digging into the muscles of my back as she pressed closer in her voracity. My erection was hard as steel, and I felt her push against me with a soft kitten-like mewling.

Burrowing my fingers into her hair, I held her head, turning it this way and that as my tongue plundered her mouth. Her own tongue circled and danced with mine as our mutual craving took hold.

"Fate ..." I wrenched my mouth from hers and buried it in her neck, burning a trail down her throat and back up again. Catching her lobe between my teeth, I bit gently, then licking it, I sucked it into my mouth. "I've wanted to do this all night."

My whisper was ragged and hoarse. Kisses, interspersed with licks, travelled along her throat and jaw before my mouth once more captured hers in a possessive kiss.

My mouth moved to the other side, and I paid it equal homage before sliding down to her collarbone and the deep V-neckline of her dress. I pulled the strap down on the other side of her arm, and her dress pooled around her waist exposing breasts encased in coffee lace, a small brown ribbon bow in the middle. Her hardened nipples strained against the material. My gaze took in her sexy bra, and I ran a finger along the top edge of the strapless lace, noting her body tremble at the action.

"God. You are so beautiful."

I looked up briefly into her eyes and saw the uncertain shyness in them. I kissed her mouth to reassure her.

Then pulling her legs away from around my body, I lifted her down to stand before me. Her dress slid downward along her body and clung to the flare of her hips. I knelt and gave a light tug on the soft material until it fell in a silky puddle covering her bare feet. My hot gaze crawled up her body, from her slender tan legs to the coffee coloured lace French knickers and matching brown bow below her bellybutton. My cock grew even harder, if it were possible.

On her left hip, nestled within the hollow of her pelvic bone, sat a small dark-red heart tattoo, no bigger than my thumbnail. Surprised, I looked up at her face. She was looking down at me, a shaky smile trembled on her lips.

"My birthmark ..." Her voice trailed away.

I recalled the strawberry discolouration. I saw it many times while swimming at my parent's house when she was younger, before she became self-conscious and covered it up. It sat just above the line of her panties, now covered by the tattoo.

"I remember." Leaning forward, I softly pressed my mouth to the red heart. It was the single, most-sexy thing I had ever seen on a woman.

I felt her shiver in excitement. Placing my hands behind her knees, I glided them up the back of her legs in a slow slide. My kiss on her tattoo deepened as my fingers slid inside her panties and my hands cupped the cheeks of her ass, pulling her against me.

I heard her gasp before her fingers twisted into my

hair and she held me to her.

Still kneeling, I licked her tattoo, my tongue laving her pelvic bone and running along the top edge of her panties in an erotic path.

When I reached the juncture of her thighs, I put my lips to her mound and breathed in her scent. Kissing her open-mouthed through the lace, my tongue licked and thrust against her wetness, making it even wetter. I smiled wickedly, my lips still pressed to her lace panties, when I heard the small, rapid panting and her soft moan as she came against my mouth.

"Oh. My. Fucking. God. Adam. What are you doing to me?"

She enunciated each word, her voice catching.

I felt her legs quiver and start to buckle, knuckles white, as her fingers gripped the counter to keep herself upright.

I chuckled. "What? You don't like it?"

"What I don't like, is that I came so fast. I wanted … You should have been inside me."

Standing, I lifted her back onto the counter. To circumvent her complaints, I kissed her again, pushing her to lie back on the counter by small degrees.

"Uh, uh. Tonight, is about you."

"Adam."

"Shush," I mock growled at her.

Faith leaned back on her elbows, her head thrown back, passion-mussed hair falling in a wild tangle of honey silk to the countertop.

She was ravishing.

I kissed the top of her breasts, easing her bra down to expose her hardened nipples before taking one into my mouth. I sucked on it, while rolling the other between my fingers. Faith arched her back, pushing them further into my mouth, while her hands held my head.

"Aahh," she groaned.

Slipping my hand behind her back, I unhooked the clasp and pulled the bra away, so it slid to the tiles. After giving the other breast equal attention, I moved down her body, raining kisses on her ribs and tummy. My fingers slipped into the waistband of her knickers and I eased them down her legs, my mouth following their progress.

I stopped when she was revealed to me. My breath caught. She had given herself an all-over tan and her skin was golden ... everywhere. She had groomed herself as well, and I was not a man who didn't appreciate her efforts. I slid her panties completely off and let them drop to land on top of her dress.

Fully naked now and lying on her kitchen counter, her hair a soft golden halo around her head and her gorgeous eyes slumberous with longing, ensnared me. I'd never seen a woman look more desirable than she did in that moment.

"Did I mention you're beautiful?"

Faith blushed.

I grinned.

I caught her hands, which lay on her tummy, entwining my fingers with hers. Using my body to spread her legs further apart, I buried my face between them.

"Oh ..." She moaned when my mouth touched her and released my hands to bury her own into my hair, holding my head to her body as she tilted her pelvis up.

My free hands now held her hips. I licked her like

she was a melting ice-cream cone on a hot day, savouring each stroke while lifting her hips to my hungry mouth, and flicking my tongue against her clit. She arched off the table and groaned aloud, her fingernails digging into my shoulders.

I lifted my head. Her eyes were cloudy and dazed with lust. Flashing her a devilish smile, I returned my attention and proceeded to taste her. My mouth alternately sucking and licking.

Sliding a finger inside her, I rejoiced as her wet warmth closed around me. Tapping my tongue against her bud, I purposely drove her closer and closer to the brink of orgasm once more. Two fingers and she was panting and writhing as she came again.

And when my tongue pushed into her, she begged.

"Holy crap, Ads ... please."

I heard Faith drag in a deep, shaky breath, her hands now pressing urgently into the counter on either side of her body.

I answered her plea, thrusting in and out until she came once again on my tongue, bucking her hips and clenching her stomach muscles.

"Oh, oh ... oh God. Yesss ..."

Faith collapsed back against the benchtop. I rested my face against her stomach and listened to her heart thumping overtime in my ear. My hand cupped her mound.

"Don't touch me please..." she gasped. "I'm so super-sensitive down there. I can't take any more."

I chuckled against her tummy.

"Three times, Faith? What a greedy girl you've become."

She attempted to laugh, but instead threw her hands

over her face.

"Bloody hell. It's been a while."

Gradually her breathing slowed. I looked up at her. Her hair had damp tendrils sticking to her forehead.

I pulled her languid body up and into my arms, brushing the moist curls off her face before hugging her to my chest, and resting my cheek on her head. I nuzzled my nose into her hair breathing in the perfume of her shampoo and some other exotic fragrance she had sprayed on.

"Give me five minutes, Adam," she murmured against my chest.

I pulled a fraction away and placed a gentle kiss on her lips.

"Faith, tonight was for you. Next time will be for us."

I bent down and picked her clothing off the floor. Shaking out her dress, I slid it down over her head. She lifted her arms like an obedient child, and the shift floated over her torso to pool in her lap.

"I think I need to go home and have a cold shower." I smiled warmly at her.

"But ... Adam." A confused frown marred her brow.

I put my finger over her lips to silence her protest, then turned and made my way to her front door, locking it behind me.

Once outside, I leaned on the wooden porch post and gulped in the humid summer air, drawing it deep into my lungs. A smile stretched across my face as I walked toward my car, curbing the urge to hobble as my body begged for release. Never before had I been inflamed to the point of pain. But tonight, was for Faith.

I knew I could have stayed the night. Made love all night long as my body and heart screamed at me to do.

But I'd sacrificed too much over the years. Too much time wasted without her, to allow me to rush it now. I'd made that fatal flaw in the past and paid dearly. Faith needed to be eased into a relationship. And if it brought me one step closer to my ultimate goal ...

Well then, I could deny myself for one night.

10

Faith

He left me sitting there on my kitchen counter. Total disbelief washed over me as my body thrummed with aftershocks from my orgasm. Make that, my orgasms.

Plural.

I waited a few minutes, half expecting Adam to change his mind, come barging through the front door, and carry me up to my bedroom.

But after I heard his car start and drive up the street, I had to put an end to my wish. I wiggled my way to the edge of the counter, noting the wetness of my climax and grimaced, but then a wide smile stretched my lips. He was a great lover. I knew he would be.

Even at eighteen he had more sexual experience than I did. Hell, he probably had more experience at sixteen.

I screwed my face up.

Why did he leave?

I jumped down from the breakfast bench onto shaky legs and scooped up my wet knickers and lace bra from the cool tiles. Walking over to the paper towel holder I reeled off four sheets and wiped myself and the counter down. Then, opening a cupboard, got out the disinfectant spray. Squeezing the trigger, I sprayed a generous amount till the stone bench top was covered and wiped it clean with more paper towels.

"I'll never be able to eat here again without thinking about Adam."

I stated the fact aloud, then slapped a hand over my mouth as though I'd been overheard. I let out a hysterical giggle.

"Oh, good Lord. I'm losing the plot."

I went to my bedroom and stripped off my dress, throwing my necklace and one earring onto my dresser. I would look for the missing one tomorrow. Not wanting to take a shower and wash off the smell of Adam and the evidence of my subsequent pleasure, I crawled under the cool sheet naked.

I even felt sexier.

Smothering a wide yawn, I clicked off the light. So relaxed and sated, my body felt as though it would melt like wet fairy floss into the mattress. I fell into a deep sleep while reliving my night with Adam and the passion which followed. Before drifting off, I promised I would not berate myself in the morning, but just enjoy the moment.

After all, it wasn't going to last.

***

I woke to noises in the kitchen and the smell of burnt toast invading my nostrils. I moaned. Scott was home. I didn't want to wake up and instead rolled over and tried to force my mind to dream about Adam. Thank God I'd had the forethought to clean the kitchen counter and pick up my discarded clothing. That could have been embarrassing.

More embarrassing than your son watching you make out on the dance floor?

I winced at the thought and burrowed deeper into my pillow.

My eyes flew open when I heard Scott outside my door.

"Mum, do we have anymore Vegemite?"

Oh God. I was lying in bed naked, my dress and underwear dropped haphazardly on the floor. My very sexy underwear.

I pulled the sheet over my body and tucked it under my chin.

"Don't come in here, Scott," I yelled out.

"Why? Have you got someone in there?" I heard the amusement in his voice.

"No. I'm not decent."

"So, you have got someone in there?" Scott gave a loud snicker at his own joke. "Is it someone I know?" His voice took on a mocking singsong tone.

Embarrassment caused me to snap grouchily. "For God's sake, Scott, I told you, no one is here. Let me get dressed then I'll come down and make a cooked breakfast."

My 'always hungry' son was pleased to be getting a meal made for him, and I heard him saunter off down the hallway, but not before he called out, "Hurry up, I'm starving."

I groaned aloud and throwing the sheet aside made my way to the en-suite bathroom. A quick look at the time confirmed it was still early morning. Plenty of time.

I had arranged to go shopping with Adam today. He'd moved into his own apartment last weekend. It was the reason he'd phoned me so late at night. At the moment he only had a few pieces of furniture he'd scavenged off his parents and sisters. He asked me to help him pick out a new bedroom suite. Was it a genuine request or did he have plans for us to become a couple? I got excited at the thought, but then forced myself to not jump to any wild conclusions.

I lathered up my hair and rinsed it off under the warm spray, wondering if it would feel awkward seeing him today. The man had given me the best orgasms of my life ... on my kitchen counter!

I was bound to feel uncomfortable. He, on the other hand, probably took it in his stride, no doubt used to it. An unexpected sharp pang of jealousy stabbed my chest. Better get used to the feeling, Faith, I lectured myself. You've chosen this path. It's not going to last ... so just enjoy the experience and try to stay friends afterward.

Adam had been out of my life for such a long time, and I didn't want it happening again. "So, harden up, you pussy." My voice echoed off the tiles in the bathroom.

My hand washed over the small heart tattoo on my pelvic curve, and I replayed in my mind the view I had of looking down at his dark head nuzzling into the dip near my hipbone. Butterflies flitted in my stomach when I recalled he said he remembered and had pressed his lips to it.

Fucking hell ... he was a sexy beast.

Whatever happens between Adam and me, I will never, ever, forget that moment, I promised myself.

Who was I kidding? I would never forget anything Adam did to me, every word he uttered, the way he looked at me, the feelings he extracted. Without question, he had effectively left his mark, and altered me in the process.

I felt so light-hearted and happy this morning, singing aloud and dancing around the room as I dressed. I paused when I entered the kitchen and saw Scott sitting on a stool at the breakfast bar only inches from where I had exploded in passion.

He looked up from his phone. "What?"

"Nothing," I lied, but felt my face flame. "Good morning." I stroked my hand over the top of my son's head and dropped a light kiss on his cheek in greeting.

A glitter on the floor caught my eyes. My lost earring. Trying not to draw attention to it, I busied myself getting bacon and eggs out of the fridge and in the process kicked it out of sight.

"So ... how was last night?" Scott asked, causing me to jump guiltily.

I turned toward my son. An evil leer was plastered on his face.

I forced my expression to remain neutral.

"It was good. You were there."

"Mum," he groaned, and rolled his eyes at me. "I mean after ... as in, last night, last night?"

"Oh. That." I turned to the stovetop, putting down

the ingredients and pulling out a frying pan from the cupboard. "None of your business."

"What?" His outraged voice had me turning to face him.

"Okay." I chewed on my bottom lip, thinking how to answer him. "Let me put it this way, Scott. How was last night for you and Michelle?" I turned the tables on him, giving a suggestive wink. "I mean ... last night, last night?"

"Eww, Mum. Okay, I get your point." He laughed. "Are you seeing Adam today?"

"We're going shopping for furniture for his new place." I started cooking the bacon. "Scott, if you want baked beans get the tin out, and the bread while you're there ..." I spied the open loaf he'd used earlier sitting next to the toaster. "Never mind."

Opening the tin and pouring it into a bowl before zapping it in the microwave, he took the hint and changed the subject.

"How about Dad being a father again? What a fucking randy old goat."

He laughed, but I sensed the hurt behind the words.

"How do you feel about being a brother? It was something you always wanted, remember?" I looked over at him as he shoved slices of bread into the toaster.

"Yeah, when I was a kid. Not now, with a seventeen-year age gap," he sulked.

I walked over to Scott and hugged him. He wrapped his arms around my smaller frame and hugged me back.

"It's going to be hard for both of us. I have to admit, I felt a pang of jealousy. All those years when I tried to have another baby and failed. I feel ... I don't know ... inadequate."

Scott pulled out of my arms and searched my face.

"Mum, you always seemed okay with it all."

"I know." I went back to the stove and turned the bacon. "I was. I just ... it wasn't right for your dad and I at the time." I shrugged. "I don't know, maybe it's a midlife crisis thing or something."

"Who cares, Mum? I doubt we'll even see Dad much anymore. At least you won't have to. I still will," he grouched.

I laughed at my son's downtrodden look. "Ha, so true. I'm sure you will love your little brother or sister when the baby comes along."

"I guess."

"Along the same lines, what do you think about Shania?"

I poured hot water into two cups with teabags and cracked the eggs into the pan while pushing down the toaster. I turned and saw Scott automatically setting a couple of places at the breakfast bar.

"She's alright, I suppose. But I feel like she's fake."

I whipped around from the stove. "Me too, buddy."

"I mean if she is so in love with Dad, then why was she trying to get Adam's attention all night?"

"Have you seen him?" I leered, flipping eggs onto our plates as the toast popped.

I walked over to the bench-top with two plates, one piled high with bacon, eggs, and the baked beans I'd poured from the bowl. The other a smaller version.

Scott guffawed. "Yeah, the dude's a fucking chick magnet."

Placing the hot toast onto side plates and making the

cups of tea I sat down next to Scott to eat.

The conversation had been conveniently steered in the direction I wanted it to go. I watched as Scott ploughed his way through a couple of mouthfuls of his breakfast before broaching the subject.

"So ... what do you think about the 'chick magnet' going out with me?"

Scott stopped chewing and swallowed. He turned, eyebrows raised, realizing the seriousness of the question buried in the casual enquiry.

A wide grin spread across his lips. "I think it's awesome."

"You do? Even though he's like, heaps younger than me?"

"Mum, you're cool. I told you, all my mates think you're hot."

"But your dad has a much younger woman and now me," I persisted in questioning him.

"You have a younger woman?" he joked.

"Smart-ass." Turning away in mock disgust, I sipped my tea.

"It's normal, Mum. Everybody does it. When I get old, I'm totally getting a young chick."

I bumped shoulders with him in play. "When did you turn into such a dick?"

"Hey, you created the monster ... now you have to live with him." Scott threw his head back and laughed.

I wanted to stay on the subject of Adam. If Scott in any way objected to our relationship change, then I wanted to know now, before it moved any further.

"What about the fact he was like a little brother to me and an older brother to you?" I queried.

"Well, yeah, I guess he was like an older brother to

me. But ..." he shrugged his look turned watchful as he paused. "Okay, now don't freak out about this Mum," Scott warned.

I held my breath for what he was about to say, putting my knife and fork down, wiped my mouth on a serviette before turning to my son. "I won't."

Scott's look was earnest, weighing up my promise before answering. "I always knew Adam was here to see you."

I opened my mouth to speak, but Scott forestalled me.

"He followed you around like a puppy and was always looking at you. Never taking my side, the prick." He chuckled then.

"He was?"

"Yeah, he was. In fact, I kinda thought of him as your boyfriend."

"What!" I squealed indignant.

Scott leaned away from me and cringed as a joke, acting as though I was going to strike out.

"He acted like it. You both did. Not when he was younger, eww, that's just gross. But shortly before he left. And when he did go - it was like you broke up with each other, and now you're back together."

I was astounded and felt my mouth drop open in wonder. Never in my wildest imagination did the thought even cross my mind that Scott viewed us in such a way. The very notion was ridiculous.

"In what way?" I challenged Scott, feeling a bit annoyed.

"Well ..." He reflected for a few seconds before answering. "What about the time he bought a new motorbike and brought it round to show you?"

"What about it?"

"I was five or six at the time. Remember, I had this obsession with bikes? If he was my big brother, he would have brought it around to show me. We would have talked about it and he would have taken me for a ride," Scott grizzled.

"Isn't that what he did?" I asked puzzled.

Scott looked at me, a rueful expression on his face.

I pulled the memory up and examined it.

Oh, dear lord. Scott was right.

Adam took me on a ride to the beach and we'd bought hamburgers and fries. We sat on the sand, laughing and enjoying ourselves, while I left Scott at his mate's place next door for a couple of hours.

Scott continued, "And all those times we went to the Warner's for a swim. Half the time Aunty Rach wasn't even there ... and Adam was always wanting to rub sun-cream on you." His face screwed up, disgusted as though we'd been having sex in front of him.

I dramatically lifted both my hands up to my face, covering my mouth in horror as the memories returned. I was sure my eyes reflected my mortification and shock as the truth of his words sunk in, losing my appetite in the process.

Shame burned into my soul. "Oh, Scott ..." I stood up next to his bar stool and wrapped my arms around his shoulders giving him a big, bear hug and pressing my lips to the side of his head. "Oh, my poor little boy. I'm a terrible mother. I should be taken out and shot. You should have said something."

"No, Mum. You're a good mother. Well, ninety-nine percent of the time. You were good friends ..." He looked at me slyly. "Maybe more. But then he left, and I didn't even know why. For a few weeks I was so mad at you."

My breath caught in my chest at his words. "You were angry at me?"

I pulled away a little so I could look into his face, but still didn't release him. My arm remained around his shoulders. "I never knew. You didn't say anything."

"I *was* angry," Scott corrected before stuffing a whole half slice of toast in his mouth and chewed on it, looking at me in a calculating manner.

"What?"

He swallowed a mouthful of tea to wash it down. "Adam came over to see you. You weren't home, and I went all psycho, blamed you, called you a bad name."

I stared at Scott. Stunned by this news. I never knew Adam had come over and spoken to my son.

"He claimed it wasn't your fault. He claimed he did something bad to upset you. That if anyone was a poopy-head it was him."

My heart felt a little stab. Adam, even then, had tried to protect me and take the blame.

"You called me a poopy-head?" I grinned.

Scott laughed. "Nah, it was shit-head actually. I thought you'd get mad if you knew I swore at six years old."

"Huh!" I gave him a light smack on his arm, and he chuckled.

He paused, and his face grew serious. "I missed him too, Mum."

I felt like a filthy piece of mould and pulled Scott in for another big hug. "I'm so sorry, Scotty. I never realized. I acted in complete selfishness, and only just now am I seeing how many people I hurt. Please,

please, accept my apology."

Scott started to squirm, feeling uncomfortable by the display of emotion. "On one condition."

I dropped my arms from around him and smoothed his floppy, sandy hair into place. "Name it."

"Tell me what happened. Why did Adam leave town?" He looked at me, curiosity in the pale blue eyes so like his father's.

I took a deep breath and let it out in a big sigh. "I guess I owe you that much." I sat back down on my stool.

"Remember what happened on the dance floor last night between Adam and I?"

His smile became salacious. "Sexy dance followed by inappropriate public tongue lashing?"

I let out an embarrassed laugh, my face heating up. "Yeah, I guess it was wildly inappropriate. Sorry." I apologized, shamefaced.

"Mum, I'm only stirring you up." He chuckled. "What about it?"

"Well ... it wasn't the first time it's happened. It took place at Adam's eighteenth birthday party. As you have pointed out, there was this ... this ... chemistry between us, even then. On my part too. Only back then, I slapped his face and said some vicious, cruel things to him. Told him I was a married woman, how dare he ... blah blah blah. Did he have to score with every woman ...? Something bitchy." I looked at my hands, ashamed. "I never saw him again. He tried to see me, but I was so angry. More with myself if the truth be known, and I refused to see Adam, or talk to him on the phone. Aunty Rachel wasn't even allowed to talk to me about him. I went full psycho."

I looked up at Scott then, my eyes begging for understanding and forgiveness. A forgiveness I didn't even grant to myself. "Anyway, he moved to Perth to live with his aunt a year later and finished university there."

"Holy shit, Mum. You are a badass." Scott whistled. "I thought it must have been something serious."

I nodded, too embarrassed to confess the more intimate details, nor my part in the whole fiasco. "But now he's back, and I ... I don't want to mess it up this time."

"I understand. It's gonna be cool. Don't worry, Mum." Scott said solemnly.

His smile turned suddenly wicked. "Two conditions now?"

I rolled my eyes at him. "Dishes?"

We laughed in unison. "Yeah, I gotta pick up Chelle."

11

Faith

Closing the drawer to the dishwasher, I glanced at the time and sighed in relief. I still had two hours before Adam picked me up for our shopping expedition. Time enough to get ready and phone Rachel.

My friend would kill me. Literally hunt me down and murder me if I didn't call and tell her how the previous evening went.

After trying on and discarding numerous outfits, I dressed in light denim jeans and a white, broderie-anglaise corset style top, which buttoned down the middle with numerous tiny hook and eye clasps. A thin white belt and sandals completed the outfit.

I wore three of the thinnest gold necklaces in varying lengths and small gold hooped earrings. After I applied a minimum amount of makeup and pale lip-gloss, I was ready to go. Strapping a white Baby G digital watch to my wrist, a spray of my favourite perfume, and a last glance in the mirror confirmed I looked groomed and confident.

I scanned my bedroom, taking in the chaos of rejected clothing and shoes. I wanted to leave the mess, but my inner neat freak wouldn't allow it. So, with a deep sigh I scrambled around hanging dresses and shirts, folding pants and even shoving shoes back into the plastic shoe rack hanging on the back of the wardrobe door.

Sitting on the back patio I dialled my friend; a glass of cold orange juice was halfway to my lips when Rachel picked up on the second ring.

"Finally. I thought you'd forgotten. So ...?"

I chuckled. "Shall I torture you the way you always do to me?"

"Don't you fucking dare."

"Oh, what's good for the goose ..."

"Come on, Faith." Rachel put on her angry teacher's voice. I knew it was a fake ploy to try to manipulate me, but I didn't care, I was far too excited and needed to share to be bothered with playing games.

"We had a marvellous night. Much better than I expected. Adam was ... well, he was fabulous." I heard my voice take on a dreamy quality and smiled.

"Wait, first tell me about the woman and Rob."

"Oh my God," I gasped. "I almost forgot. She's pregnant."

"Get fucked."

Rachel's words elicited a chuckle from me. It was so Rachel.

"No, seriously. First of all, her name is Shania ..."

"Like the singer? Shania Twain?"

"Yes, only she's younger and prettier ... if you like gorgeous blondes with blue eyes - which I don't anymore ..."

"Ahem," Rachel interrupted.

Being a gorgeous blonde with blue eyes, she was righteously upset.

"Haha, Rach, present company excluded of course. Plus, I'm sure she's a bottle blonde. The white-blonde kind with those big, round boobs -implants!" I confirmed knowingly, sipping the juice I had been holding for the last few minutes. "And defs on the Botox, although why the hell she would bother at twenty-something is ridiculous."

"Well, you would know being in the beauty business. Okay then, all is forgiven."

I heard sounds of the kettle boiling and her making a hot drink.

"So, she's got the fabricated hair and tits. What else? False lashes too, I bet."

"Am I on speaker?" I asked.

"Not anymore."

"Good, cos there's a bitch-fest coming, and it's for your ears only." I wriggled my bum more comfortably on the cane lounge chair.

"Fire away."

"She's an accountant in his firm. The firm her father owns." I stressed that last part, knowing Rachel would think like me. It was easy to get ahead on your rich parent's coattails. She would also know my ever ambitious, career-climbing ex-husband would factor it into his affections.

"Convenient," sarcasm dripped from her words. "Trust Rob."

I snorted in agreement. "She's so fake, and so far up her own arse, she could probably give herself a colonic cleansing with her own tongue."

I heard Rachel give a bellow of laughter. "Oh, shit ... I spilled my coffee on me. What did Scott think?"

"Scott says she's okay, but he thought she was a fake, too."

"She's pregnant, huh? Explains the wedding announcement then," Rachel stated, a bitchy tone in her voice.

"Thank you. That's what I said. In my head, of course." We laughed.

"Of course." There was a long pause and then. "It would have hurt, given your pregnancy history."

I loved how Rachel and I always agreed on almost everything, and she understood me so well.

"Yeah, well ... that goes without saying. It's my kryptonite for sure." I felt a slight misting in my eyes but pushed it away. "Rob knew it would upset me, which is why I think he wasn't planning on revealing the news last night. He looked surprised himself when she blurted it out."

"So, she told you?"

"Not only me, she told everyone at the table at the same time. Just 'boom' ... no subtlety."

I heard the outrage in my voice.

"Do you think he told her about you not being able to conceive and it's why she did it?"

"No doubt about it," I claimed disgusted. "I'm kinda

happy for Rob. He always wanted more kids. And I did too, don't get me wrong. I just ... just ..."

"Didn't want them with him." Rachel supplied my missing words.

I was speechless. Did she realise after the whole 'the kiss' incident, I found it so damn difficult to get turned on by Rob? We seldom had sex. And when we did, it was more a duty thing - I can acknowledge it now. We spent years living this sham of a marriage.

"We tried, Rachel. You know that. But yeah, you pretty much summed it up."

"I know, Faith, but you didn't seek any medical help did you?" she asked.

I was silent for a while. The thing I loved about Rachel, she was brutal in her honesty and always hit the nail on the head. It was also the thing I hated about her.

"No." It had taken me years, but I finally admitted it out loud. "I didn't want to bring a child into a loveless marriage. I mean after all a baby was not going to save it."

"Which is why I can never understand why the hell you wanted him back."

"I don't know." I rubbed the bridge of my nose in confusion. "I'm fucked up, I guess. It was the right thing to do for Scott. It was ..." I searched for the perfect word. "Safe. Comfortable. Predictable."

"Boring," Rachel finished.

I gave an awkward laugh. She was right. It was tedious.

"Anyway, it's finished now," she stated. "Moving forward ... what did Adam think?"

I blew out a breath of relief, glad to change the

subject.

"He didn't like her. But, as to be expected, she was all over him, grrrr." I allowed the green-eyed monster to make a brief appearance.

"I can't imagine Adam bothering with her when he had you," Rachel said with confidence.

Good on you, Rach, I beamed into the phone. "No, he didn't. In fact, he defended me. He was so sweet, Rachel."

I spent the next thirty minutes updating my friend all about the dinner, and how Adam had purred up to me all night. I also related our sexy deja vu dance, and how Rob and Shania had left in a huff.

"Ha serves him right. And what about when Adam took you home? Was there any rumpa pumpa?"

I was picturing Rachel waggling her eyebrows and thrusting her hips in a suggestive mime.

"There was a bit ... but he didn't stay the night." I paused. "I don't feel comfortable going into detail, Rach, you being his sister and all. It would be just ... eww, it's not right."

"I agree. But was it good?"

"Oh, yeah. It was the best orgasm I've ever had in my entire life. All three of them." My voice took on a husky tone in memory.

"La la la la la ...." She sang aloud into the mouthpiece. "Too much, Faith."

"Oh. My. God. Who knew Rachel Crane could be embarrassed?" I chortled.

"Well, he is my half-brother. And even though you pretend he's yours ... let me tell you now, sweetheart, he was never, I repeat, never, your brother. You two just played the silly game."

"I'm beginning to comprehend that, at long last."

"Did you see the tattoo?" Rachel asked, jumping to another subject.

"No? Should I?"

"Well, if you had sex, you would have."

"It's a long story. It wasn't sex, sex." I felt awkward trying to explain to my friend the nature of our sexual encounter.

"Okay, well, when you do, be prepared to freak out."

"What do you mean?" I asked.

"Never mind." She raced to change the subject. "Did he see yours?" Rachel asked.

I was happy to comply, especially to this one. "Oh, Rachel, he was so adorable. He remembered ... he remembered my hideous birthmark."

"Uh huh, thought so."

"And he kissed it ... he licked ..."

"Hey!" Rachel yelled. "Enough, for fuck's sake."

"Oops, sorry."

My best friend changed the subject before I could say any further intimate things about her brother.

"Are you still coming to the movies with us today?"

I had promised to go and see 'Beauty and the Beast' with Rachel and her twin daughters, Chivon and Sacha. I loved the girls almost as if they were mine. Today there was a special screening, with all the little girls dressing as Disney princesses. Rachel's mother had made the girls' dresses and together they had done their hair and makeup. I would have loved to do it for them but didn't want to steal the attention from Julie.

"Of course, I wouldn't miss it. What time?"

"The 5:45 session," Rachel called out absently. She sounded like she was looking it up on her tablet.

"Mum's not coming. She's got rehearsals."

Rachel and Adam's mother, was a keen actress in amateur theatre, performing in plays with the local drama association. I was glad she wouldn't be in attendance, not ready to face her, now that Adam and I were spending time together.

"I'm going shopping with Adam. We're buying furniture for his new place, so 5:45 is perfect. We can go to dinner after, if it suits you?"

"Ooh look at you, shopping like a married couple," she teased. At my groan she continued. "He is so nesting."

"No." I wanted to stop her in her tracks, before she blew things into something more meaningful than they were. "He admired the way I'd decorated my place, and he asked me to help him, that's all."

I heard a snort on the other end of the line. "Oookay."

"It's true."

"What? I said okay. I'm agreeing with you."

Her words agreed with one thing, but her tone. Her tone was a sarcastic bitch.

"Let's not get our hopes up here, Rachel. It's only been one night."

"Nooo of course not. One night, and ... what is it ... eleven years?"

I gave a loud sigh and ignored her comment. From experience I knew she wouldn't let it go. And the more I denied, the harder she would dig in.

After a few seconds of silence, she grouched, "You're no fun. Alright, dinner sounds good. Now I don't have to cook dinner ... yay."

"Lazy bitch."

Rachel chuckled. "And proud of it. I'll buy the tickets online, so we don't have to queue and pick you up on my way through."

12

Faith

"I love this mattress." I looked at Adam in the bed beside me.

We were in the bedding shop and this was the third mattress we'd tested. It was a king-size ensemble with storage drawers in the base and a pillow top mattress. It was like sleeping on a marshmallow.

He gave me a wicked sensual smile. "I think we need to test it out properly."

I couldn't help but smile at his dirty mind. "Here? In front of everyone? Didn't last night on the dance floor satisfy your exhibitionist streak?" I joked.

"I meant let's jump on the mattress. Why, what did

you have in mind?" His innocent eyes ran over my face. Then he wagged a finger at me. "Stop trying to corrupt me, you hussy."

I giggled and sighed. I hadn't felt this happy in a very long time and was having a ball going shopping for Adam's bedroom furniture. He allowed me free rein to choose whatever I liked. I didn't need my arm twisted. I chose a dark wood and leather combo four-piece suite, which consisted of chocolate brown leather bedhead with wooden posts and no foot-end, two dark wood bedside tables and a matching tallboy. Now all that was left was the mattress.

"It's too soft." Adam stated. "I'd sink and drown."

He rolled over to my side of the bed and I felt myself leaning into the dip his weight caused. "Oh, I see what you mean."

He touched a finger between my eyes and slid it down the bridge of my nose to the tip. "I want to kiss your nose," he stated.

"No."

"But it's so adorable," he pleaded.

"No. What happened at the other shop?" I spoke in feigned anger.

"You put a spell on me and made me kiss you, and then you got embarrassed when the salesperson cleared his throat and gave us a dirty look," he murmured shamefaced.

"Exactly. Except for the spell part."

"This time will be different," he promised.

"You mean different as in the kiss won't be passionate and involve your tongue?"

He scoffed. "Of course, I'm not going to stick my tongue in your nose."

"I wouldn't put it past you," I grumbled.

He leaned over and dropped a kiss on my nose, anyway. "See."

"Ahem."

We both looked up in a mixture of surprise and shock, then promptly burst out laughing when a saleswoman stood over us.

"Is there something I can help you with?" She gave us an indulgent smile.

I slid away from Adam, swivelling to the side and dropping my feet onto the floor. "We love this bed but it's a little on the soft side. Does it come with a firmer mattress?"

"There's one down the back, but it's in a queen-size. We can order a king-size in for you." The woman started to walk toward the back of the shop, expecting us to follow.

I made a face at Adam. He slid over to me and we raced to catch up with the woman.

Two hours later we purchased the mattress with the guarantee it would be delivered later in the week. Since the rest of the furniture wasn't arriving till the end of the week, there was no rush.

We'd also bought a couple of sheet sets, pillows and a quilt, plus other sundry items for the bed. Adam purchased two bedside lamps and a rug for the bedroom floor, before the final stop at an electrical shop for a flat screen TV and a digital clock/radio.

"I've had enough shopping for one day. Come back to my place. You can check it out and get an idea of what things you think I should buy for the rest of the apartment," Adam suggested. He pulled my arm through his while pushing the trolley out to his car.

"I'm dying for a cup of tea," I agreed.

***

Adam's apartment was gorgeous. Almost brand new, it sat on the second floor in a low-rise complex. Modern and spacious, with light wooden floorboards, it had big sliding glass doors, which opened out onto a generous balcony overlooking the harbor. The view drew me, and after dumping the bags, I moved out to inspect the scene below. Rows of boats moored against narrow jetty walkways, lined the protected waters. Below was a wide paved footpath, dotted with concrete planters overflowing with scented shrubs.

Underneath and to the left, was a popular cafe, busy at this time of the afternoon with tourists and Sunday diners catching the late afternoon sun.

I made my way back inside, joining him in the kitchen where he had set up the kettle. The room was white and pale grey with a stone bench top and stainless-steel appliances. A huge, brand new silver fridge looked large squeezed into the recess provided.

"Very nice." I nodded my approval, perusing the pantry in my search for tea bags while he pulled two mugs from the overhead cupboards. The TV was placed on a lonely coffee table in the lounge-room.

"You don't have a microwave?" I pointed out the obvious in the empty nook above the wall oven.

"On the list for next week."

Adam grabbed two bags and headed through a small door into a tiny hallway. Motioning for me to follow, he gave me the guided tour.

Only three doors came off the hall. One into a

bathroom, one into a spare room and one into his master bedroom.

The spare room stood almost empty except for a lone ironing board and iron. Two electric guitars stood propped against a large black amp. I recognised his red and white electric Fender he'd had for years, but a much newer, black version had joined the small collection. There was also a black guitar case lying closed on the ground nearby, which no doubt housed an acoustic.

He dumped the bags containing the Manchester on the carpeted floor. The bathroom next door consisted of a shower, sink, and toilet in shades of pale grey. Again, it looked unused.

The main bedroom contained a rumpled, unmade double bed. The metal pipe work screamed cheap eighties. The size of the room made the bed seem tiny.

"Wow, nice size room," I remarked.

"I know, right? It's one of the things I liked about the place, plus the fact it also has double doors, which open out to the balcony."

I walked over to the doors and without opening it, looked out. The lounge room shared the same view. Thick block-out vertical blinds pushed to one side stopped the morning sunlight from wreaking havoc on sleepy eyes.

The room had two doors, one led to an en-suite bathroom, the other a walk-in-robe. "Very nice, Warner. Two bathrooms. I likey."

"I think so. All the stuff we bought today will look good in here, don't you agree?"

"Very good." My eyes lighted on the unmade bed and I pictured the new bed and furniture in the spacious room. Unplanned, my naughty mind envisioned myself and Adam lying across the new bed, limbs entwined in the throes of passion. I swallowed thickly. "How's my cup of tea going?"

We drank our tea on the deck. The apartment came with a cheap round metal table and two chairs. I imagined how hot the metal would have been earlier in the day when the sun was at its peak, but now it was starting the slow slide down in the west, the balcony was shaded.

"You should get some better furniture for your terrace and maybe some plants," I suggested.

Grimacing, I looked at my watch. My day with Adam was almost at a close. "I have to go soon. Rachel is picking me up from my place at five. We're taking the girls to the movies."

"Oh, anything I might like?" Adam asked. He looked as though he was considering joining us.

I chuckled. "Beauty and the Beast. It's a special 'princess screening'."

He scowled. I laughed harder.

Picking up my cup, I took it to the kitchen. Going down the hallway I used the bathroom. I still had a few minutes before I had to leave so decided to make his bed for him.

"What are you doing ..."

"Nearly done." I was fluffing up the last pillow when he walked into the room.

"I would have done it. Eventually," he laughed.

"I know. But now you don't have to."

With one knee on the mattress, he reached across and grabbed my hand pulling me until I toppled onto the bed with him.

"There's no salesperson now. So, I can kiss you without interruption," he said and proceeded to do so. He kissed my eyes, my brows, my nose and started to poke his tongue into my nostril.

"Noo," I giggled, turning my head away.

His mouth latched onto my cheek and worked its way to my lips, where he kissed the corner of my mouth. His fingers turned my face to him, and his eyes held mine. My heart flip-flopped, and I went very still at the look in his. Passion. Pure, unadulterated passion, burned in their depths, turning his azure eyes almost black. Sensual, mesmerizing and so hot, it burnt right to my core. He gave me a slow, sexy smile, and I turned to mush.

Good lord, but he was potent.

His mouth captured mine in the most enticing kiss. His tongue grazing my lips before sliding in tentatively and meeting the tip of my own in a light touch, tasting mine. His fingers caressed my jaw, sliding down to rest against my throat, cupping my neck while his thumb stroked the hollow where my pulse throbbed.

With his eyes gazing into my own he deepened the kiss, slanting his mouth over mine while his tongue pushed deeper, twining with my own. I closed my eyes and gave myself over to the hunger I felt growing between us.

Adam's mouth moved down my throat, his fingers now deftly unhooking the many clasps on the front of my top. "As sexy as you look in this top, babe, please don't ever wear it again when you're with me."

I snickered. It was ridiculous how he was able to make me laugh, when all I wanted to do was have him buried inside me.

He dropped kisses along my chest above my top as it was slowly opened, revealing the white bra beneath. When he'd completed the task, he pushed the sides of the stiff corset-like material to either side and looked at my breasts encased in the thinnest silk.

Next, he pulled the straps of my bra down my arms, the material of the lingerie followed. I heard a soft groan before gentle fingertips caressed my taut nipples. They ached for his touch and I found myself involuntarily arching myself in offering to him.

Eyes closed, I unconsciously held my breath and savoured the feel of his hands as they cupped my taut mounds. I pushed up into his hands like a wanton and gasped when I felt his searing mouth close around a tip. With both hands on the one breast he pushed it up to his mouth and laved the nipple before sucking it into his greedy mouth.

I felt myself start to squirm as shooting electrical charges went straight from my breast to between my legs. My fingers dived into his hair, holding his head to my chest. My hips lifted and pushed against the hardness I could feel pressing against my leg.

Adam lifted himself up a small degree, moving inches to settle over me, and pushed his erection between my legs. My eyes opened to look at him in a sexual haze. How had I ever thought I could ignore the things this man made me feel?

He moved his attention to my other breast, giving it the same treatment and driving me to arousal. A direct link running from my sensitive nipples, straight down the middle of my body and ending in stimulating currents sending bolt after bolt to the core of my sex, had me pushing myself into him. He felt my need and mirrored it by grinding against me.

My hands pressed into his shoulders, my nails no doubt making small crescent shapes through his black t-shirt and into his back as I gave a soft moan with my need. He lifted his head from me and looked into my eyes, a puzzled look in his face.

"Adam, I ..."

"Shh." He put his finger to my lips.

A knock sounded at his door. Adam rolled off me.

I looked down my body. My top was unbuttoned and pushed to the sides, my bra pulled down around my middle, the straps clinging to my upper arms. Breasts laid bare, with nipples hard and aroused. The gold necklaces pooled in the middle of my chest.

Then I looked at Adam in horror. His hair was messed, courtesy of my craving fingers, his shirt wrenched out of his black jeans. When had I done that? And his erection straining at the fly.

"Uncle Ads?" young voices chorused.

Our eyes met in dread.

"I can't answer the door like this." He sat up, swinging his legs over the side and groaned, motioning to his hips.

Appalled, I leapt off the bed, yanking my bra up and hastily hooked up my top as I raced to the front door, neatening up my hair as I went.

"Just a minute, sweeties," I called out to my friend's daughters. I looked at my watch. 5:10 p.m.

Oh fuck, oh fuck, oh fuck.

I swung the door open.

"Aunty Faith." Two little princesses launched themselves at me.

I bent over and cuddled Rachel's daughters. "Whoa

125

... you're like twin tornadoes."

After the girls hugged me, they twirled around for my inspection. They both giggled and dropped into a curtsey.

I curtseyed back. "Oh, my goodness. I wasn't expecting royalty this afternoon."

"I'm Belle," Chivon announced proudly. She was dressed in the bright yellow dress from the ballroom scene.

"Aunty Faith, I'm Cinderella." Not to be outdone, Sasha preened and pointed to her glass slippers, which I'm sure were plastic.

"You look so beautiful, ladies. I wonder if Prince Charming will be there?"

Scrunching up their faces, they said, 'Eww yuk,' in unison, before suddenly turning their attention to scrambling out onto the patio.

Rachel wasn't as annoyed as I expected her to be for being late. My friend smirked at me, pointing to my chest. "Nice look."

Scanning down at my top, I threw a sheepish grin to my friend. I had hooked it up wrong. It was bunched with one side longer than the other.

"Holy crap." I twisted away to the kitchen and using the pantry door to conceal myself, undid the hooks and readjusted my blouse.

"Where's your partner in crime?" Rachel snorted, watching my dressing antics.

"Right here, Rach." Adam bounded over to his sister and gave her a quick kiss on her cheek before going out to the girls on the balcony. I heard their shrieks of delight as he scooped them up into a bear hug.

"Sorry, I got side-tracked ... let me grab my bag and

we can go." I flashed her an apologetic grin.

"So, I see."

Hearing my friend's sarcastic comment, I made a face at her.

Snatching my bag off the kitchen counter I raced to the bathroom, using the toilet, before a quick freshening up of my makeup and a combing of my messed hair back into place. A cursory glance at my mobile phone confirmed I had missed the two phone calls Rachel had sent, plus the three text messages:

STILL ON FOR THIS ARVO? GIRLS ARE PUMPED.

LEAVING NOW. SEE YOU IN 5 MIN
.

CALLED ROUND BUT YOU'RE NOT HOME YET. PICKING YOU UP FROM ADS. BE READY BY 5PM.

When I returned, Rachel had joined Adam on the balcony. He was pointing something out to her daughters who laughed with hysterical abandon at whatever he had said.

"I'm ready ..." I called out and started singing the Beauty and the Beast song for the girl's benefit, since I knew how excited they were.

They both squealed and ran back in.

Adam joined in the frivolity by pulling me into his arms and waltzing around the empty dining area. His rich baritone voice causing the girls to giggle as he continued to re-enact the scene from the cartoon when Belle and Beast were dancing around the ballroom. Of course, his voice was infinitely better than mine.

We danced past Rachel and he let go of me and

swept his smiling sister into his arms. The girls screamed, so thrilled to see their mum dancing.

We were all laughing when he stopped in front of the girls and performed a courtly bow in front of them. "May I have this dance, my ladies?" he asked before sweeping them both up into his arms, one on each side and twirled around the room once more. He started singing the few lines he knew.

Rachel came over and stood by me, a smile twisting her lips. "How on earth does he know the words?"

I shook my head negatively, beaming at his antics and the eight-year-olds delight with their uncle.

Adam performed a final twirl and deposited the girls onto the couch. He must have overheard Rachel. "You two made me sit through it a million times when I was a kid."

We laughed uproariously, remembering how it was Rachel and my favourite cartoon as young teens. That and Aladdin were the go-to cartoons on babysitting duties.

I laughed now as I relived the memory and how he had scowled earlier when told what movie we were planning to watch. No wonder he didn't suggest joining us.

***

I looked up at the clock on the wall – 1:00 p.m. The day was quiet and dragging. I'd only three customers booked in for the rest of the day, although walk-ins were common on a Friday afternoon. Standing behind the cash register, I stared with blank eyes at the open drawer. I was supposed to be organizing my banking and cash for the weekend, but my mind was on other things.

I can't believe today marked only two weeks since Adam had returned to my life. It seemed as though the eleven-year gap never existed. We had slotted back into a comfortable relationship. Too comfortable and too easy. I felt as though it was just too good to be true and was waiting for the other shoe to drop.

I hadn't seen Adam since Sunday afternoon when we were interrupted by Rachel and her daughters. I chuckled at the memory of him dancing with his nieces. He was so good with children.

"What's so funny?"

I looked up from the till. My co-worker and friend, Cat, stood on the other side, finished with her customer and ready to finalize the sale.

"Oh, nothing. Sorry, just daydreaming." I smiled to the customer. "Oh, the colour suits you, Mrs. Renwick. Much better. It's such a soft tint."

Mrs. Renwick, who'd coloured her brows a dark brown for years, was in her sixties, and the lighter grey tones were so much more flattering to her pale skin.

"Thank you, love. Cat's done a marvellous job." She ran her fingers over one brow.

I stepped away so the transaction could be completed before waving goodbye.

"Quiet for a Friday." Cat plopped herself down on one of the leather couches in the waiting area on the other side of the counter. There was only the two of us in the shop. Outside it was hot and humid, the threat of a thunderstorm looming.

"You were thinking about him, weren't you?"

I felt my face turn soft and whimsical. "Yeah."

"Oh man, you are so in love." She smirked.

"No. I love him, true. I've always loved Adam. But in love...?" my voice trailed off.

"Oh, okay. I see what's happening here." She wiggled her fingers over my body like she was casting a spell. "You're in the denial stage."

"What? Noo."

The phone at my elbow trilled, making me jump. I answered, "Faith in Beauty. How can I help you?'

"You can help me by christening my bed tonight."

Adam.

"It's been delivered?" I turned my back on Cat, so my friend couldn't see the complete joy I was sure was on my face at hearing his voice.

"Not yet. It's getting delivered this afternoon. I'm finishing up here at three and meeting the delivery guys at my place. Wanna knock off work early? We can sort out the bedroom and have dinner downstairs."

"Umm ..." I turned around and looked over at Cat, wondering if I could talk her into staying and closing up. Cat worked four days a week, Friday to Monday. She covered the quiet days, Sunday and Monday alone, so I had a two-day break. With a small toddler, it suited her to be at home most days and work when her husband and mother took turns to look after her daughter.

Cat now had a big smile plastered to her face. She batted her eyelashes, and with both hands over her heart, mimicked a fast beating pulse.

"I'll try. Let me check with my 'staff' and text you back," I said, having a dig at Cat who continued to tease me. Now she was fanning herself with her hands and making goo-goo eyes.

"Okay, try hard." His voice got lower, like he was at work and trying to be discreet. "I've missed you this week. I'm looking forward to test-driving the new bed with you."

I turned my back once more to Cat as a light blush heated my cheeks at my friend's blatant eavesdropping. I swallowed hard. "Me, too," I croaked.

"He's sexy talking, isn't he?" Cat called out, laughing outrageously.

I covered the mouthpiece and turned back to my friend, shooting daggers. "I have to go ... sorry." I hoped Adam hadn't heard Cat.

"Alright, see you soon."

After he hung up, I glared at my friend.

Undeterred, she questioned, "I was right, wasn't I?"

I couldn't be angry at Cat. I was too happy and light-hearted to be mad at anybody right now. "Yeah. He's bought a new king-size bed, and it's getting delivered this afternoon. He wants me to test it out with him tonight."

"Oh my God. You so have to." She squealed jumping up from her position on the couch. She started bouncing around the shop like a twelve-year-old, singing out of tune, *"Someone's getting laid tonight ... someone's having fun ..."*

I couldn't help but smile at her infectious made-up song.

"Is it okay if I leave early and ..." I didn't even get to finish my question before Cat chimed in.

"Hell yeah, as long as you name your firstborn after me."

"You idiot," I laughed.

13

Faith

I'd left work early as planned, and after a quick shower had changed into a pale-yellow cotton dress. Although the air was stagnant and the heat oppressive, I still teamed it with a light short-sleeved blouse left hanging open, and white rubber thongs on my feet. When I'd arrived at Adam's place he had not long come out of the shower, as evidenced by his damp hair. He, too, was dressed casually in denim jeans and a white T-shirt.

Together we moved the bedroom suite into position, placing the lamps with new bulbs onto the bedside tables. Adam hooked up the television on the tallboy, while I put new, crisp beige sheets on the bed, leaving the quilt for a cooler day. The room looked luxurious with the new furniture and I was pleased with my choices.

After an early light dinner in the cafe and a stroll, we planned to go back to his apartment. I was on edge with excitement, the true reason for my visit keeping me on pins and needles for the past few hours. Although it wasn't late, a storm was brewing off the coast and the approaching bad weather had brought on an early darkness.

We walked hand in hand along the boardwalk and down to the end of a large jetty, nodding to passers-by and two old men fishing off the end of their boat, which was tied to the mooring. We stood in companionable silence, Adam's body pressed to the back of mine, both arms wrapped around my shoulders, his chin rubbing cat-like on the top of my head. We watched the lightning of the incoming storm dance across the black sky and heard the thunder rumbling loudly.

Adam was recounting an incident at his work this week, which had consumed most of his nights, working late to get the drawings submitted to the planning commission by the deadline. So engrossed in his story, the sudden crack of thunder accompanied by the onslaught of rain had me squealing, and we ran hand in hand along the jetty and the last few metres into the apartment building. The cloudburst fell in big fat plops, marking our clothes in polka-dot splotches and soaking our hair.

Laughing like a couple of teenagers while shaking off the rain, Adam went to fetch a towel. When he returned, I was standing by the open balcony door watching the water sheet straight down; the sound of the storm loud and exhilarating to my tightly wound senses.

I had peeled off my white blouse and was standing in just the yellow cotton dress, made see-through by the water. Adam wrapped a thick white towel around my shoulders and rubbed his hands down my arms to dry them. Turning me, he dabbed at my hair and face with the edge of the towel, his own hair still dripping slightly.

"What about yourself, silly?"

I pulled the material from around my shoulders and stood on my toes to wipe across his forehead and blot at his hair, made black by the wetness.

His eyes deepened colour rimmed by wetly spiked lashes. They gazed intensely into my own before moving to my lips. I watched a drop of rainwater escape from his hair to slide down his face and perch precariously on his top lip. I leaned forward, my tongue reaching out and licked it from his mouth, drawing a soft moan from him. He closed the tiny gap, his lips touching mine softly. They were cool, and he smelled of tropical rain and the musky cologne he always wore, the fragrance an aphrodisiac to me.

Adam took the towel from my limp hand and dropped it to the floor, deepening the kiss, his mouth hungry. Pushing me urgently up against the wall his large hands cuffed my wrists above my head, his body boxing me in against the cool plaster.

He pulled away abruptly, and I watched his beautiful mouth shape harshly whispered words. "Do you know I have waited my entire adult life for this moment? Spent years watching you ... wanting you, Faith. Torturing myself with visions of you before I went to sleep at night. Waking up hard and hungry."

His fierce eyes were drugged with desire, the blue irises hidden beneath the dilated pupils. Hot need smouldered in their depths, willing me to understand and feel his craving. Sensual tremors passed unseen from his body into mine, causing an erotic thrum between my legs.

Adam pushed his face into my neck, his tongue sending liquid lava racing through my veins as his mouth burned a molten pathway up from my shoulder to my ear, where it stopped to make a husky promise. "No more waiting, Faith. Tonight, you're mine, and we will finish what we started so many years ago."

A flash of light and the deep rumble of thunder dramatized his words. I drew an unsteady gasp, reminding my lungs to breathe. I felt the slight sandpapery scrape of his cheek resting against mine before he moved to capture my mouth once more. His lips, demanding in possession ground against mine, our tongues twined and danced to a carnal beat of their own making.

His large muscular body pressed even closer, forcing my softness to flatten and yield to his commanding frame. One hand moved down an upraised arm, encircling and caressing as it glided over the smooth surface, cupping my shoulder in a brief stroke then moving downward in its exploration.

The other hand continued to hold my arms pinned above my head, although there was really no need. I wasn't going anywhere soon.

His mouth moved from my lips to shower kisses over my face. Cheeks, nose, eyes, jaw. Nothing was left untouched by his wonderful crooked mouth, as the seductive deluge continued in a downward pattern back to my lips.

Emotion filled his eyes. They locked onto mine, sharing a lingering look before his sharp teeth took gentle possession of my bottom lip, drawing it into his mouth for more starving kisses.

Tearing his mouth from my own, he teased me with hot, sucking kisses down my throat, his tongue caressing the hollow at the base. A hot, needy quiver raced down my spine.

Inserting a long finger beneath the strap of my dress, he followed its lines, slowly pushing the thin cotton fabric of the dress down until one silk-clad breast was exposed for his inspection.

My nipple tightened, pushing against the thin material and begging for his attention. He didn't disappoint. His fingertip stroked the hard nubbin which seemed to swell even more. The hot achy feeling caused me to arch my back in response, inviting further examination.

I watched as his hand cupped my breast, curling around the fullness of the soft mound, feeling its weight and measure before squeezing gently and massaging.

Oh, God, I was on fire.

Instead of easing the aching tension, it only intensified tenfold. A soft moan escaped unintentionally from my lips, and I twisted against the restriction of movement, rubbing against his hardness.

"I know, babe," Adam soothed, before his mouth descended to take a silk enclosed nipple deep into his hot mouth.

Flames of desire were licking up my body and swirling all around as he sucked. Slow at first, then harder as one hand tore free from their confinement to grasp his head and hold it in place.

Looking up into my passion induced eyes, he chuckled wickedly. "Easy, Faith. I'm not going to stop."

I focused onto his amused face, surprised to see my hand buried into his dark hair, clutching a fistful in my fingers. Giving him a sheepish look, I released my death-grip on his locks.

He dropped a quick kiss onto my swollen lips before pulling my bra under my straining breast and resumed his magic. His free hand lifted its prize to his mouth, the flesh soft and aroused. Need ripped through my body as his mouth closed around the now exposed nipple and suckled. Every part of me was alive with sensation.

Releasing my other arm, his fingers entwined with mine as he brought it down to his side. He pulled the straps of my dress and bra on the other side down to hang at my elbow, displaying my other breast for his scrutiny. Adam flicked his tongue over the hard peak, drawing out an identical response from my pleasure-drugged body. Then taking it into his mouth, he sucked on that bead too, until they both stood stiff and erect.

Releasing his hair, which I had unconsciously buried my fingers into once more, I slid my hand across his shoulders and back, fingers biting into him in ecstasy when he drew passionately on me, causing a dynamic jolt to shoot to the juncture of my thighs.

Lifting his head, he slipped a strong leg between both of mine, creating a sawing motion to ease my ache.

Never had I felt this lust-driven need crawling through my body like fire-ants, making my legs weak and my body want to squirm. My heart slammed against its protective cage my breathing laboured.

I sensed the same urgent need in Adam, but knew he was taking it slow for my benefit, controlling the powerful urges gnawing at both of us.

His hand slid up along my thigh, taking the thin cotton fabric in its journey. A warm palm cupped my hip bone, sliding over the sensitive curve, before gliding across my lower back to slip beneath the silk of my panties and over the smooth curve of my cheek, pulling me hard into his arousal. My leg lifted and wound around his.

"Mmm, you feel so good, so smooth and hot." His husky words were whispered against my lips before his mouth took possession once more.

Deft fingers traced down along my rear crease until it reached its goal. My own burning arousal greeted him, it's wetness testimony to my desire. A long finger caressed my dewy folds before making a gradual entry to slide, slick and deep, into the waiting warmth.

A soft gasping moan tore from our joined mouths as I pressed down onto his hand, my back bowing in my excitement.

"Oh, Adam ... I ... I pleeease." I could feel my control slipping fast and was on the verge of climax, my body wound up so tight.

When he pulled out his finger and deliberately added another, pushing both silkily back in. It was too much, sending me over the edge, my body clenching with my climax, my moisture coating his fingers.

"Omigod ..." I got out between pants of breath.

Adam rested his lips against my forehead while I sucked in deep breaths, willing my pulse to slow. I would have fallen had I not been held up between his body and the cool wall. His mouth brushed against the damp curls at my hairline.

When he spoke, his voice was an unsteady rasp. "My new bed is calling out."

Reaching down, he pulled my leg up over his hip. Once it was resting there, he reached for the other and did the same until he was wrapped by my legs, my thongs left forgotten on the floor. Cupping my bottom within his palms, he pushed up off the wall walking with me down the hallway toward his bedroom as I clung to his shoulders.

Although I had only moments before climaxed, I could feel my arousal building once more with the erotic sensations such an intimate position caused. The feel of his denim clad stiffness rubbing against the juncture of my thighs was sending my senses into overload. His mouth latched onto mine as we made the sexy journey, my arms wound tight around him, our tongues duelling.

Adam set me down beside the bed, my legs unwinding with careful deliberation to gradually support my own weight. His arms slid around my back, and I heard the soft zzz of my zip sliding open. Unerringly, he opened the clasp of my bra and, in one smooth motion pulled my dress, bra and all, down the length of my body, until I was standing in my white panties.

I stood before him in all my near-naked glory, a light breeze from the open balcony door cooling my hot skin. The light from the half-closed door of the en-suite cast a muted glow to the room and bathed my body in it.

Kneeling at my feet, Adam pressed his head against

my stomach, bestowing hot open-mouthed kisses over my tummy, a hot, wet tongue making circles around my navel. Shivers of delight raced up and down my body as his arms held me before him, one arm wrapped around my bottom and thighs, the other gripping my hip in a warm palm.

His mouth moved lower still, licking and laving my hip bones and swirling into the hollow of my pelvis, giving scant attention this time to my tattoo, moving on to more important erogenous points, while sending fiery bolts to ignite between my legs. My hips arched in instinctual carnal invitation.

Adam's mouth came to a stop, resting on the barely-there nest of curls hidden beneath the silk. His voice sounding deeper and thicker than usual with his arousal. "Faith ... I want to taste you again."

Heat pooled between my legs at his words. "Oh God, Adam, yes ... yes."

My hands were now holding his head, my fingers twisting into the dark softness, unconsciously pushing his head lower to fulfil the promise of his kisses.

Pushing me with gentle hands back onto the bed, Adam ran his palms up and over my thighs, gliding over their silky smoothness and parting them with unhurried passion before sliding my panties down off my legs. He looked at me lying before him, smouldering heat igniting his gaze. Feeling open and exposed I felt a dull flush creep up my skin.

"You're gorgeous," he breathed, before he lowered his mouth to me.

He made love to me with his mouth and it was the most wonderful experience of my life. It's not as if I had never been loved in this manner before, even taking into account the other night. But this was different. It was an eruption of sensation and emotion all rolled into one, an explosion which blew apart my world and altered the landscape of it forever.

He lapped, he licked, he laved. Alternately sucking and kissing. Big open-mouthed kisses, hot and wet, and luscious, and wicked. Flames of desire coursed up my body. Lightning bolts zapped and cracked with electrical charge, the storm inside the bedroom mimicking and competing with nature's version outside.

I writhed and moaned, torturing the sheet with Chinese burns, pulling and twisting at the cotton as my hips bucked. My breathing became harsh and strained, and my heart once again slammed against my ribs. I could feel the crescendo of another orgasm building.

"Oh hell ... Adam," I gasped. "I want you inside me. Please Adam, now." I pleaded, I begged, I demanded.

Reaching down, I grabbed handfuls of his T-shirt and yanked hard. Sitting up, I leaned across him, pulled the shirt from his waistband on his back and jerked it up over his head in a frenzy of haste.

Catching onto my frantic need and feeling it too, he stood, kicking off his shoes and almost tearing the fastening from his jeans, shucking them in record speed. Peeling off his underpants, they went as well. I had little time to admire his delicious body and other assets before I felt the glorious weight of his body as it covered mine. Giving up the fight for self-control, he plunged full hilt into my wet warmth.

Together we groaned in sheer pleasure from his deep thrust. My internal muscles stretching to accommodate and caress his thickness in welcome.

Our gazes meshed in mutual rapture. Adam pulled out and then oh so gradually slid back inside the silky cavern. Every inch of him stroking deep inside me.

He started to thrust, long and deep, in and out, until we were both panting, our bodies slick with sweat. His tempo built up faster and faster, pumping harder. My hips instinctively lifting up off the mattress as I caught onto his rhythm.

The pressure built, pushing us closer and closer toward the edge of our control. With one final deep and penetrating drive, he pushed us both over the brink. I wanted to scream, but instead bit my lip to hold back and thrashed my head while clutching at his shoulders, crying out his name as a soul incinerating climax shattered me. My nails pressed little moon shapes into his skin with my release, internal spasms clenching and tightening around him, milking the very essence from his body as I wrapped my legs around his hips and held on.

Adam arched his back in climax, shuddering with the force of his orgasm, sweat sheening his body.

"Aaah ..." His groan was harsh and guttural.

His body collapsed against me. His heaviness an erotic, momentary weight which was pleasant.

"Fate ..." he mumbled, between raining kisses onto my damp forehead.

He rolled over while still inside me, taking me with him and holding my body close to his, my head on his shoulder. I felt the pounding of his heart slow against my own and felt him burrow his nose into my hair.

After a few recovery minutes of lying collapsed against each other, Adam slid a hand under my chin, lifting my head so I was looking up at him. "You okay?"

I only just noticed the rain had eased to a light patter, tapping on the concrete balcony, the muted thunder echoing in the distance.

"No ..." My voice was a breathless whisper. "Am I alive? I think I died and went to heaven."

He chuckled, and I saw his beautiful, gorgeous, talented mouth split into a crooked grin, as he allowed his head to fall back against the mattress.

Sitting up straddling his hips, I leaned over and dropped a light kiss on his contented looking mouth. I pulled myself off him and ran my gaze over his now nude body, noticing he was still semi-hard. Either that, or he was getting aroused again.

"Seriously, Ads, I always knew you would be a great lover, but jeez ..." I froze mid-sentence.

When I'd sat up, a crack of light from the bathroom door slashed across his perfect body, highlighting a tattoo I hadn't noticed before in the frenzy of mating. It lay across his chest, over his heart. One word in calligraphy writing.

Fate

I'd forgotten about the tattoo Rachel mentioned, and now as I sat next to him, I reached out and with delicate fingertips traced over the writing. My eyes caught his, and I saw the quick flick of fear in them and felt the complete stillness of his body. My own eyes filled up with emotional moisture and a single drop slid from the corner of my eye to roll slowly down my cheek as realization hit me.

Adam loved me.

14

Adam

I watched as a single tear wound down Faith's cheek. She leaned forward and kissed me lovingly. It was the sweetest kiss we had ever shared, transmitting emotion, but I hoped not sympathy.

I felt the moisture on my face from her tear, and realized she was aware of the symbolism of my tattoo, and the truth of my dark secret. But I wasn't ready to lay bare my love ... No, make that, Faith wasn't ready to hear me confess my feelings and desires, and I was too afraid full disclosure would scare her off.

She straddled me as the kiss deepened, and my hands slid up from her hips to cup her breasts as she sat on me. I would never get enough of her, and I felt my cock, which had not lost its strength, harden against her. She rubbed herself against me and moaned. I pulled her forward, taking a nipple into my mouth. My hands cupped the cheeks of her ass, massaging the globes and pulling her up to sit atop my erection.

"Yes ..." her voice was breathy as she sank down, her hot wetness stretched to encase my shaft.

"Ah ... that feels ... so ... fucking good." My words were broken, my voice rough with desire.

I started to pump, but she stopped me with a hand on my chest, and with her eyes holding mine in a hypnotic gaze, she leaned forward to kiss me with passion. Then using her leg muscles, lifted herself enticingly slowly up off my cock, her internal muscles gripping and clamping around me as she rose. Before she could pull out altogether, she lowered herself and repeated the exercise, her hands braced on the mattress above my head for leverage, the motions like an erotic caress. Her throaty moans of pleasure making the sensual undulations even more of a stimulant.

Fucking hell, she is literally milking my cock.

"Babe, I'm not gonna be able to hold out if you keep doing that." Was that my voice all raspy and ragged?

"Oh ..." she stopped, sitting up then smiled. A naughty, sexy smile. "I kinda like the fact I can push you over the edge."

She stretched her body, raising her arms up in the air, then brought her hands down to her breasts, cupping them and stroking them in a provocative tease.

I groaned loudly, and her smile grew bigger. She grabbed my hands and brought them up to cup her breasts with hers on top, and together we caressed her.

"Oh, you're a bad girl," I growled.

She laughed wickedly.

Her hands dropped to either side of my head as she leaned forward, her chest on mine. Her lips rested on mine and I felt the words against my mouth while she continued her seductive pull on my shaft.

"Well, bring it then, Warner. Fill me up with your hot cum. Let me coax every drop out."

"Jeezus ..." Her words were like a trigger, and with both hands clamped to her hips I lifted my own and drove into her. Once, twice, before bucking for a final thrust and calling out in a hoarse climax. "Aah ... Faith ... fuck me."

I collapsed back against the bed.

"I just did, lover."

I laughed shakily, pulling her down to me.

"Did you?" I questioned if she had climaxed.

"A little one. I owed you."

I turned to my side pulling out of her and padded to the bathroom. Cleaning myself with a handtowel I brought it back into the room for her. Then climbing onto the bed and taking her with me, I repositioned us, so our heads were on the pillows. Facing her, I looked into her eyes, my own studying her familiar features, loving her so much. I watched the subdued light dance across her face and placed one hand to rest on the side of her cheek, cupping it.

"I didn't use protection."

She shrugged.

"No, I mean ... I never not use protection," I stressed.

She gave me a soft smile. "I trust you to not have any diseases. And it's not like I'm going to get pregnant."

"You might."

Faith shook her head negatively. "No, Adam. That's very unlikely given it was hard enough to get pregnant when I wanted to. I had to take my temperature every day and work out the exact time when I was ovulating. Even then it didn't work. No, I'm not a breeder."

"What about Scott?"

"An anomaly for sure. A blessed anomaly. But an anomaly just the same."

"You had a couple of miscarriages though?" I remembered how upset she was about them.

My fingers played with her hair, rearranging it around her face before finding an appendage to play with. I stroked her ear and pulled on her lobe.

Her eyes darkened in remembered misery. "Precisely my point. If by some miracle I got pregnant, I'm sure I wouldn't be able to carry it to term."

My eyes roamed her face as she talked, absorbing the different expressions which flitted across it. I leaned forward and dropped a light kiss on her forehead. I didn't like to think about the pain she had felt and wanted to chase away the memory.

I couldn't stop touching her and gave up resisting, stroking her lips with a thumb while gazing into her eyes, feeling as if I could drown in their golden depths.

Wanting to make it up to her for any pain I had caused, I spoke softly, apologetically. "Faith ... I know I messed up before, messed up big and lost you." Needing to explain and reassure her, I sought to find the right words. "But this time is different. I'm more mature. Last time I ... I was selfish. I wasn't sure. I didn't know what to do. I knew you were married, and I knew you didn't want me the way I wanted you. I promised myself I would keep my hands off you.

Promised myself I would forget you and move on ... but it was a promise I couldn't keep. I had to go away. There was no way I could stay here and not see you." My eyes pleaded for her understanding.

Her lips trembled in a thin smile. "Shh no, Adam." Her fingers covered my mouth. "You're wrong. I did want you. Too much. It's why I was angry. I felt so guilty for wanting you and so turned on by you at the same time." She gave a quiet, unsteady laugh. "God, you were so sexy and ... and hot. I felt like a dirty pervert. A dirty, married pervert."

I leaned up, pushing her onto her back, my face above hers, my hands on either side of her head. "I felt like I lost everything when I lost you. I kept remembering I had let you down. That I let myself down too. And picturing the disappointment on your face. It was pure torment. The past can't be undone. But maybe this time, I won't let you down." My eyes held hers, beseeching. "This time I want it all, Fate. I need you back in my life."

Her eyes filled up with moisture. "I want it too, Adam," she said, and pulling my head to hers gave me an intense kiss in answer.

***

I smiled to myself in the dark. I was tired, but reluctant to go back to sleep. Looking down at the woman nestled to me, I still marvelled she was mine. I wanted to run out onto the balcony and shout it from the rooftop, but I'd probably get cursed. Faith was meant for me. Every piece of her fit every piece of me, like some crazy jigsaw puzzle.

The problem was convincing her of the fact. Tonight, I had taken one step closer, but I wasn't confident enough to believe it was the final step. I still felt she was holding something back. I was holding back, too. I longed for the time when I didn't have to. No more pretending. No more bullshit. Just Faith and me.

Lying here looking at her, I picked a strand of golden hair, which had stuck to her lips and with care so as not to wake her, pushed it back to join the rest of her hair spread out on the pillow in a tangle. I thought back to the years of angst after I grudgingly realized I was in love with her. Seventeen at the time, young and immature, but not so young I didn't recognize the signs. Jealous of each smile, each touch she gave to her husband. Every time I saw them together, I'd die a little more.

But I was also full of cocky arrogance, sure she felt something too, and it was only a matter of time before she acknowledged it and ran away with me. I couldn't confide in anyone. My mates would have thought I was nuts, and Rachel would have scolded me for sure.

When I wasn't with Faith, I questioned my feelings, berating myself for my fantasy. But all of my doubts melted away when I saw her. It was her eyes. They were an open door into her soul. They confirmed my belief she shared my feelings.

Youth had made me impatient, and I acted too soon and lost her. Then I ran away like a sulking child. To lick my wounds. Wounds that wouldn't heal, no matter how much time I gave them.

Soon after arriving in Perth, I recklessly tattooed her name across my heart, confident she would always hold a place there. And she had. No other woman could replace her or fill this emptiness I felt when she wasn't in my life.

I'd wanted to come back and claim her as soon as Rachel told me she had separated. This time though, I was patient. I knew she wasn't ready. So, biding my time, I made plans to return home and claim what I always felt was mine. I hoped this second chance would bring our hearts together.

I snuggled into her warmth. Luxuriating in the amazing afterglow making love to her brought me. I allowed it to wash over me like a magical feeling that soaked into my soul. I've never felt this swept away by a physical union. I snorted to myself. Who was I kidding? This was much more than physical. It was almost spiritual.

She murmured in her sleep, rolling over so I could spoon her. I smiled to think I'd wasted money on a king-size bed when we only took up a third of the mattress. Averse to moving my body away from hers, even if it was for sleep, I curled up into her, pulling her softness against me as I closed my tired eyes. Even unconscious, some part of my body longed to touched her. I fell asleep with this thought circling my mind.

15

Adam

"Tell me again why we have to visit your parents?" I leaned into Faith sitting beside me in the departure lounge at Melbourne's Tullamarine Airport and nuzzled into her neck.

She scrunched her shoulders up and giggled. "Quit that. It tickles. You know why. We've been together a few months now, and I didn't want to tell them about us over the phone."

I watched as she tapped out a text message to her mum, explaining we were running a bit late due to bad weather. We'd caught a flight down from Townsville to Melbourne, hoping to connect to a smaller plane to

Launceston in Tasmania, but were delayed for a few hours.

"You're too kind, sweetheart. I can't believe you honestly think they would give a shit."

She looked up at me then, not at all offended by my remarks about her parents. "Oh, I know they won't care. But at least I'm doing the right thing, even if they can't support me with it. Or rather, they aren't interested."

I shrugged at her words and she went back to typing her message. I could never understand nor get my head around Faith's weird relationship with her parents. Her mother and father were dyed-in-the-wool hippies. Or the modern-day equivalent of 'alternative lifestyle choice people,' or whatever the hell they called themselves in the twenty-first century.

They'd lived for years in a commune on the New South Wales/Queensland border until Faith's mother became pregnant and they moved into the house she'd inherited in Townsville, across the road from my family.

Faith acknowledged and even accepted the fact she was a mistake. Her parents were quite open about it. Especially her mother, Jean, who never wanted to be ruled by the patriarchal society, which relegated women to the role of mother and caregiver. She believed in freedom and felt children hampered her lifestyle choice. Both parents were artists, and they expressed their down-to-earth personality through their artwork.

Poor Faith was often left to fend for herself, while her selfish parents immersed themselves in their 'creative calling' as they put it. After Faith, they had made sure, through a medical procedure, the reproductive error wasn't repeated. As an only child, she would have been lonely if it weren't for Rachel, and subsequently my parents, who became her surrogate family.

An announcement came over the speakers, and Faith cocked her head to listen. "That's us."

She tapped my arm and bent to pick up her small carry-on luggage. We would only be there for two days, so we'd brought a limited change of clothes.

"I've organised a rental car for the weekend. We'll pick it up at the airport then drive down to the farmhouse."

I nodded my head at her words as we moved along to the front of the small queue, handing our boarding passes to the steward.

In my opinion, Faith's parents were complete wackos who used excuses to pursue a hedonistic life, free from certain responsibilities. She accepted them as best she could and reluctantly came to visit them annually out of a sense of duty. Faith was big on doing the right thing. Needless to say, I was here to support her.

"It's so weird to be taking off and then levelling out for a few minutes before the plane starts to drop altitude for landing." She smiled at me in excitement as the plane's wheels started to lift off the tarmac.

I looked at her happy, smiling face. "I'm just grateful it's a short flight. I simply want this weekend to be over with."

She rolled her eyes at me well aware I didn't have much time for her parents. "Jean and Jonah will be so surprised we're together," she stated.

Faith always called her parents by their given names. Mum and Dad were pronouns they didn't adhere to.

"Do you think they'll even remember who I am?" I asked.

"Of course." She bit her lip. I knew it was a giveaway sign she was doubtful as well.

Her parents had been so narcissistic their entire lives, I questioned if they'd even noticed the neighbour's kid in their self-absorbed world.

"We'll see."

***

After picking up the small Ford Fiesta we'd rented, we drove north from Launceston to a small farming community along the River Tamar. It was an apple orchard Jonah had invested in, purchased with the sale of their Townsville home years ago. Faith's father was originally from Tasmania and longed to return to his roots. He had a range of organically grown apples, which were processed into boutique cider. It wasn't hugely successful, but combined with Jean's handcrafted jewellery, the two businesses kept the pair comfortable.

I drove up the long gravel driveway and parked outside the front of a small cottage in a wide dirt parking area. A sign with an arrow pointed to the back where the cider sales office was.

Jean stood on the front veranda to welcome us. A couple of scruffy brown dogs barked erratically at the car, while three cats sat in various positions along the railing, looking down on us haughtily. Faith looked at me, a bright smile stretching her mouth, a happy sparkle in her eyes.

I couldn't stop myself from brushing the back of my fingers along her cheek in affection. "You go ahead," I said. "I'll get the bags out of the boot."

"Okay."

She grabbed her purse and stepped out of the vehicle to be instantly surrounded by the dogs. They squirmed around her in wiggling joy, jumping up in greeting as she struggled to get past them to her mother.

Too busy with Faith, they hardly noticed me as I pulled the bags from the back. I watched from the rear of the car as she mounted the stairs and was embraced by her mother; the maroon beret she wore on her head, the only colour on the dark veranda.

A short, pudgy older man walked around the side of the building, a stiff-legged gait to his stride. The dogs noticed me when the closing of the boot alerted them to my presence, and the barking frenzy started again as they raced toward me. The man, who I guessed to be Jonah, and who I hadn't seen in years and barely recognized, shooed them away and ambled toward me, his hand outstretched.

"You must be Faith's friend?"

I shook his hand. "Jonah, good to see you again."

He looked at me in surprise, dropping my hand, his eyes squinting behind the wire-rimmed glasses.

I knew it. He hadn't a clue who I was.

I looked over at Faith on the veranda, but she was busy chatting with her mother.

Jonah wore a grey plaid flat-cap hat and a khaki parker coat. Underneath, he wore a black, knit jumper and grey trousers that had seen better days. Large black gumboots, stained with mud and clumps of grass clinging to the wet rubber, completed the outfit. He now took off his hat and scratched his head in thought, in what I remembered was a habitual gesture.

"Are you the fella she brought with her last time?"

What the hell? Faith's brought someone else to meet her parent's?

"No. I'm not sure who she brought before, but I'm Adam Warner. I lived across the road from you as a kid. You probably remember my sister, Rachel."

His eyes lit up. "I remember Rachel for sure. She practically lived at our place."

Hmm not quite true. In reality, it was Faith who lived at our place. But I let it drop. "Yes, well, I'm her brother."

I looked to the front of the house and guessed Faith was telling her mum the exact same thing when I saw Jean look over at me with a puzzled expression. I lifted a hand in greeting. She gestured back, but her frown grew more baffled.

***

Later at night I cuddled up to Faith in the double guest bed. It was inadequately small, but I wasn't complaining. It meant I spent the night plastered to her body.

"Bloody hell, it's cold," I grumbled.

My lips moved down her throat as I kissed my way to her shoulder. She arched her neck to allow me easier access.

"Mmm you smell good. Mind if I eat you?"

She giggled at my words. "Surely you're not still hungry after your big meal?"

I lifted my head and looked at her face incredulously. "You could have warned me your mother's cooking tasted like shit."

Faith burst out laughing. "I thought you'd remember."

"I vaguely remember you telling me, but I'd never experienced it in real life. No wonder you were always eating at our place."

"Shh, they might hear you." She giggled again. "Thanks for leaving some bread for me by the way. You didn't have to eat the whole loaf on your own."

"Yes. Yes, I did." I went back to kissing her shoulder. "Fuck knows how your old man is so chubby."

Faith snorted. "He's probably got a secret stash out in his shed. Notice he spent half the day there?"

"By the way ..." I rolled her over so she was lying on her back and my lips could move down her chest to my actual destination, her breasts. "I won the bet. You owe me. I told you they wouldn't remember who I was."

"We didn't bet, did we?"

"I did. In my head I bet if you won, you could have your way with me. But if I won, I could have my way with you."

I pushed her singlet to the side, pulled a stiff nipple into my hot mouth and felt her catch her breath.

"Oh." I heard a small gasp. "Now I remember," she sighed.

I felt her push her fingers into my hair and hold my head against her breast.

I lifted my head up when a disturbing thought occurred to me. I looked into her eyes, seeing the passion in their unfocused depths.

"And who the hell did you bring with you to meet

your parents' last time?" I felt a flare of jealousy. It was completely unreasonable, since Faith was entitled to bring anyone to meet her parents since we weren't together, but it pissed me off all the same.

Her expression became confused. "Last time? I ... just Scott."

I stared at her. "Surely Jonah isn't stupid enough to think I'm his grandson?"

Faith pulled out of my arms slightly and put some distance between us, pulling the sheet up to cover herself. "What do you mean? What did Jonah say?"

I grimaced, wishing I had never brought this up. But since I had ruined the mood anyway, and I wanted an answer, I continued. "He asked me if I was the same 'fella you had brought last time."

A frown marred her brow in thought, then cleared after a few seconds. She burst out laughing. "Oh, good grief. Jonah thought you were Scott's mate, Damien." She sank back down into the bed and giggled. "Are you jealous, Ads?"

Her sharp eyes watched me, a mischievous twinkle in them.

I gave a self-deprecating smile. "Maybe a little."

"Aww, babe, come here." She pulled my head down to her and kissed me on the lips. Pushing my head up, she put a hand on either side of my face and smiled softly at me. "It's my job to be jealous of you."

"Yep, agree," I said. "I've spent enough years feeling jealous to last me a lifetime."

I leaned down and started to kiss her hungrily. Just the memory of all the times I was envious of her husband made me want to enjoy the woman here now.

Faith wrenched her mouth from mine. "Wait a

minute, does that mean my parents think you're one of Scott's friends?"

I saw the uncertainty and fear start to cloud her eyes.

"No. God, no." My lips captured hers again. "Do I look seventeen?" I asked the words against her mouth. "Is this the cock of a boy?" I pressed my erection against her hip but didn't wait for a response. Instead, I pushed my tongue into her mouth and did my damnedest to make her forget this conversation.

It worked.

***

"Darling, you know me. I'm all for women having younger men. Life's too short, Faith. You have to grab hold of whatever pleasure you can and run with it." Jean lifted a silver necklace from her workstation. "Now, this piece for example. I put all my passion into it. Just last week a young man in Canada contacted me on my website and insisted I make it for his girlfriend."

How the hell it had anything to do with Faith having a younger man was a puzzle. I scoffed under my breath. My guess was she wanted to talk about herself and slotted it into the conversation.

Looking at Faith with her mother I saw where she got her good looks from. Her mother was a smaller, older version of Faith. Her once golden blonde hair, which I remember from her youth, was now mostly white, and she had hazel eyes. She'd aged, her shoulders had hunched over a little, which made her look even thinner than she was, hollowing out her belly.

I noted her hands were thin and bony, covered in sunspots as she held the jewellery out for our inspection. Jean insisted on wearing the long flowing gowns and flared genie pants, which dated back to her younger days, when she was part of the hippie counterculture and rejected mainstream ideology. Which of course in this case included up-to-date fashion. She would have to be cold in her leather sandals, shuffling about in her workspace, which was actually a converted back shed.

I listened half-heartedly while Jean gave us a tour of her studio. She was talking as if I wasn't even in the room. I knew I should have gone with Jonah into town, but I wanted to spend every available minute with Faith.

Did I come across as too needy?

Maybe, but a part of me worried Faith's parents would say something callous to upset her, and I'd installed myself as her protector.

Jean turned to me then, her eyebrows raised. I'd somehow tuned out of the exchange once she'd started to prattle on about her jewellery, so missed the gist of the conversation.

"Sorry?" I snapped myself back to attention.

"I hope you're not expecting children, Adam? I think Faith's childbearing days are well and truly behind her, hey honeybee?" She touched Faith's shoulder and gave it a squeeze. "It's not as though she was popping them out all over the place, anyway, thank goodness. One child is enough, I think. This world is getting overpopulated."

Faith looked to the ground, but I saw the stricken look she tried to hide sweep across her face. I moved behind her and hugged her, wrapping my arms around her shoulders. Holding on tight, I rocked her in my arms.

Fuck. Fuck. Fuck. Fuck. Fuck.

Jean moved on to her next piece she wanted to show us, babbling on about herself, oblivious to the grenade she'd just dropped.

"I'm happy with just Faith," I stated emphatically.

Jean turned back to us.

"Of course, you are. She's an angel. It's why we called her Faith - unquestioning belief and trust. That's our girl."

Faith's mother didn't even notice she'd upset her daughter. Throwing a bright smile at us, she moved on to her favourite subject.

"Did I tell you Launceston Art Society contacted me about showing some work?"

I switched off Jean and focused on Faith. I whispered into her ear. "Are you okay?"

She pulled out of my arms and turned to me. "Of course," she smiled brightly. She put on a brave face, but her wavering smile gave away her true feelings. "Why wouldn't I be?"

Faith might be a better actor than I gave her credit for, but she sure the hell wasn't fooling me. I knew she was upset and fighting it, but now was not the time to discuss it.

In half an hour we would be heading off to the airport. Once safely back home I could broach the subject.

16

Faith

"**H**as it been four months already?" Rachel flopped down on the charcoal mesh poolside lounge chair. Pushing her wet blonde hair back from her face and sliding on dark glasses. "It's gone by quick."

"I know."

Taking a long swallow from the iced lemon drink, my fingers wiped at the condensation on the side of the glass. We both lay sunning ourselves poolside in Rachel's backyard, the girls playing in the shallow end with their mermaid dolls.

"How was Tasmania? And the old witch?"

We cackled together. It was a standing joke between us. Rachel referred to my mother, who she'd once spied doing an incantation spell in my backyard; from that day she'd always called her 'the white witch.' She wasn't of course. My parents were just alternative in their choices and beliefs. They followed their own mixed up belief system, whereby all forms of theology had something worthwhile to contribute to society. Everything from Christianity to Pagan rites was considered acceptable.

There had always been a tension between my mother and my best friend. Where Rachel's mother and family had been, well ... like family, my parents were a different matter. Something which irked Rachel and subsequently Adam as well.

She had never approved of the relationship between my parents and me. Far from perfect, I had accepted it a long time ago. Their new-age attitude and honesty had always made them completely transparent.

Maybe if I didn't have the Warners living across the road, life would have been far lonelier. But whenever my parents were too preoccupied in their artistic pursuits to provide dinner, I knew I could always eat at my surrogate family's table.

"It was interesting."

"What? They didn't approve?" Rachel had her back up in an instant, ready for a battle to protect her friend and little brother.

I put a hand on her arm. "No ... no. Nothing like that. You know what they're like, a couple of narcissists. 'That's nice, dear, now look at this wonderful new piece I'm working on'." I mimicked my mother and her self-absorbed obsession.

We both laughed. "What about your dad?" Rachel asked.

"Jonah was the same. I don't know why I bothered going down there to tell them. Some masochistic sense of duty, I guess. As usual, they weren't interested."

"But ...?" Rachel looked sharply at me.

I looked at my friend and scowled. She knew me too well. "Jean said something that upset me."

"I knew it ... the cow." Rachel sat up and swung her legs around the lounge chair and lifted her glasses to scrutinize me. "About Adam?"

"Yes."

"Spit it out."

"She said ..." I hesitated before qualifying. "And it's just something I've already thought about. She pointed out I can't give him children."

I frowned. Rachel didn't explode the way I'd expected her to. I chewed nervously at my bottom lip. "It's crossed your mind too, hasn't it, Rach?"

She didn't answer for a long time. Tears pricked in my eyes hidden behind the dark sunglasses. Good lord, I really needed to toughen up. I was turning into this fragile snowflake waiting to melt at the least amount of heat.

"I'd be lying if I didn't say I've never thought it. You've seen how good he is with my girls?" She looked apologetically at me.

"He would be a wonderful father," I agreed sadly.

"But, Faith, that's his call. I mean it's not like he's asked you to marry him, Has he?"

I shook my head.

"You know he's in love with you?" Rachel stated matter-of-factly.

"I know. He hasn't voiced the actual words, but I can see it in his eyes, and of course there's the tattoo." I acknowledged my friend's attempt to make me feel better.

"You love him, don't you?" Rachel asked.

"So much." I threw a wobbly smile at her. "Why I fought so hard to deny it even to myself, I'll never understand."

"It's the way you were brought up," Rachel stated. "All that 'free love' shit had the opposite effect on you. You've lived your life as the ultimate good girl. Sticking to the rules, always the responsible one. Kind, courteous, caring. It's time for the 'rebel' to emerge, Faith." Her passionate speech ended with an upraised fist.

"I want to. God knows I do. But I also want to do what's best for him." I closed my eyes and willed the stupid, hot tears away. I took a deep, calming breath before I voiced the next words. "And I'm not what's best for him."

Rachel didn't disagree with me. Instead, she placated me with words of appeasement. "See where it goes, Faith. Don't stress over nothing."

Rachel slid back around, swinging her legs onto the lounger, and grabbing some sunblock, she squeezed a dollop onto her palm and rubbed it into her shoulders. "At least wait until you're married before you start worrying about children."

I put my glass on the table between us and using the excuse of lifting my red baseball cap off my head and smoothing my wet hair back, I wiped at the tears which had escaped their watery pool.

"I know. It's all the female attention he gets. I'm

finding it hard to deal with as well." I turned worried eyes to Rachel.

"Really? It's not like you haven't been seeing it our whole lives."

"I guess." I chewed on my fingernail. I hadn't done that since I was a teen and mentally chastised myself for reverting to my nervous bad habit. "It's different now that he's my boyfriend."

"Well, stand up for yourself. Use your smart-ass attitude I taught you."

I laughed at her words. Rachel was the queen of 'comebacks' and had attitude by the truckload. She was always giving me tips on how to put people back in their place with just a look or some well-chosen words.

"You're right. That's what I'm going to do."

"Good girl." She gave me a double thumbs-up gesture. "I knew all those years of training you would pay off," she snickered.

"It won't be easy. I mean, he can have anyone. He's gorgeous, kind, funny, successful. Perfect really," I sighed, feeling depressed. "No wonder they fall all over him. The only negative thing is he's not filthy rich, otherwise he's every young girl's dream,"

"He's rich," Rachel stated.

"I can't understand ... wait. What?" I snapped my head around to the lounge chair next to me.

"His dad's sister, Marissa, left him a truckload of money."

I stared wide-eyed at Rachel.

"He hasn't told you?" she questioned.

I shook my head, speechless.

Rachel sighed loudly. "Okay, but you didn't hear it from me. Act like you don't know, when he does." She sat forward, her voice turning conspiratorial. "So, Pedro's sister, the aunt Adam went to live with in Perth, went back to Italy. Remember, I told you she let Adam live in her house for like super-cheap rent while he went to university?"

Rachel always called her stepfather, Peter, 'Pedro'- even though his actual name was Pietro. Named by his Italian mother, who married an Australian.

I shook my head negatively for the second time in as many minutes. I knew Peter and his sister were both born in Australia, but his mother returned to live in Italy when her husband passed away. Marissa lived in Perth and doted on Adam, so it didn't surprise me she allowed him to live almost rent free.

"Well, anyhoo ... while there she had this affair with a rich Italian businessman." Rachel leaned over to have a slow sip from her drink on the table beside us.

I gritted my teeth, here we go - cruel bitch. I'd just have to be patient.

"Anyway, he bought her a seaside villa on the Italian Riviera. They'd meet there for their amorous trysts. About five or so years ago, they both died in a horrific car crash - it caused quite the scandal."

"Oh, yeah, that's right." I put my hand to my mouth. "Your family went to Perth for the funeral. I remember you telling me it was a car accident, but I assumed she'd passed away in Australia."

It was around the time Rob was talking separation. It didn't surprise me I hadn't paid too much attention; I was consumed with trying to put the pieces back in the mockery of my marriage.

"Well the thing is, she left Adam as sole beneficiary. The villa was worth a few million. Well, a few million

Euros anyway. Not sure what it was in Aussie dollars. Plus, the house in Perth, which he rents out. It was in an upmarket riverside suburb as well."

I whistled. "What about Monique or Peter?"

"Nope, only Adam. I met her once. He is the spitting image of her. She didn't have any kids so ..." she shrugged. "Plus, he went to Europe and stayed with her for a month or so."

Rachel and I didn't talk about Adam much over the years after 'the kiss' incident. I was starting to realize there was a lot about him I didn't know.

"Why am I only hearing about this now?" I questioned.

Rachel turned disbelieving eyes to me. "Are you kidding me? If you remember, every time I brought up the subject of Adam you claimed you didn't want to know."

"I know I did. But I meant I didn't want to know if he was dating, or getting engaged or worse still, getting married. I asked you about him." I looked at Rachel who was shaking her head.

"Yeah ... stupid things. Did he still play in a band? Had he finished his Architecture Degree? Did he like living in Perth? You never asked anything personal," Rachel scoffed at me.

I turned outraged eyes on Rachel. "That's not true. I asked you if he was happy."

I remembered how hard it had been for me. It was probably a year after he had moved away, and I was miserable. I'd had a couple of miscarriages. My marriage was failing, and I was struggling to keep it all together. If it wasn't for Scott, I probably would have called it quits years earlier. To make matters worse, I couldn't stop myself thinking about Adam every so often, even after two years.

"You told me he was very happy," I reminded her.

"He told me to say that if you asked." Rachel looked a bit shamefaced. "I didn't like being in the middle of you two."

"Okay, fair enough." I allowed her the concession. "It must have been difficult for you."

"I'm not surprised he didn't tell you about his inheritance. He doesn't talk about it much since Monique missed out. I don't think he wants to get her jealous or anything," Rachel said.

Monique was Rachel and Adam's younger sister. Although she looked very much like Adam, that's where the similarities ended. She didn't have his charisma or sweet personality. She tended to be vain with her looks, discarding boyfriends often. It didn't help she was spoiled by her parents and took advantage of it.

Only two years younger than Adam, she had been away in the USA for the past two months and had returned a week ago. As yet, I hadn't caught up with her. Although we got on well, it wasn't the same as my relationship with the other two siblings, and I always felt she resented me for it.

"Wow. Yeah, I can see how she'd be pissed. So, did he buy his apartment? I thought he was renting."

"It's his."

"Oh ..." I tapped my chin with my French-manicured fingernail.

Rachel chuckled. "You sound disappointed he's rich?"

"I think it's wonderful he's rich. But bloody hell, it just makes him too good to be true. I'm fucked." I threw myself back into the lounge-chair.

"Aunty Faith, you have to put money in the swear jar." Sasha stood over me, a big smile on her face.

I clapped a hand over my mouth. "Oh sorry, sweetie, Aunty Faith is a naughty girl."

17

Faith

The following day I was in the laundry room throwing wet clothes into the basket to hang out. I usually reserved my Mondays off for housework and errands. It was late afternoon, and after this load I was planning to throw a salad together and barbecue some steaks for dinner.

"Knock, knock." Rob popped his head around the corner, a smile on his face.

"Robert, what are you doing here? How did you get in?"

"I'm here with Scott. He's upstairs getting changed. We're going to get new rims on his car."

I nodded in remembrance.

"I wanted to say g'day. How's things?"

"All good." I was suspicious of his question especially since I hadn't heard from Rob since after the initial dinner when I'd met his fiancée. As predicted, he'd called the following day and lectured me for setting a bad example for Scott. We didn't part on the best of terms. "Why?"

"Just being polite, Faith," he accused, making me feel mean for doubting his sincerity.

"Oh." I felt I needed to make some personal query in return. "How's Shania and the baby? A little girl I hear?"

Rob's smile grew wide and a dreamy quality entered his eyes. "Yes, we still can't agree on a name, but everything is going along as well as can be expected. She finishes up work in a month. Taking the last trimester off, so now it's a waiting game."

"I thought you would have married straight away?"

He sighed. "I wanted to, but Shania wants to wait until she's lost the baby weight."

"What baby weight? She looked skinny when I saw her last."

"Nah, she's got this cute little belly now." I could see the love in his eyes and a strange part of me was glad for him.

"I'm glad you're so happy, Rob. I hope it all works out for you." I smiled but was to regret my words only seconds later.

"What about you? Are you still with the toy boy?"

"Toy boy?" I frowned annoyed. "Excuse me? You're one to talk. I think there's a bigger age gap between you two than there is with Adam and I."

"There is, but it's more acceptable - hell, it's high-fived among men." He looked at me with a phony pitying glance. "With women, well they usually come across as a desperate, try-hard."

Fuming at this stage, I put my hands on my hips in a fighting stance. "I'll have you know it's not as uncommon as you make out. There're loads of couples where the woman is older." I stabbed my finger in the air at him.

"True, but are you going to be always wondering if he's with another woman whenever he's late home from work? Or, if in ten years' time, when you're middle-aged and he's in his prime, if he's looking at your grey hair and wrinkles and thinking he could do better?" Rob smirked.

The fucking bastard. Acting all nice. Two-faced backstabber.

"Of course, I'll think that. Won't you?" I countered.

A smug expression crossed his face. "Not really. I just made junior partner in the firm, so I'll be providing her with the lifestyle most women want. My wife won't have to work. She can afford to buy designer outfits and go on overseas holidays. Have more children. What do you have to offer Adam?"

I stared at him open-mouthed.

Don't cry. Don't you fucking cry.

"Get out." My voice was low and filled with seething fury.

"Faith ... now don't get upset." He started backing out of the small laundry room. "I'm helping you to face reality, before you make an even bigger fool of yourself."

"GET THE FUCK OUT!"

Rob turned and fled. I would have laughed at the comedic image he provided had I not been so upset. Seconds later Scott came skidding to a stop in the doorway.

"Mum?" A worried frown creased his brow.

I turned away from him, not wanting him to see the tears, which filled my eyes and threatened to escape. I was desperate to blink them back.

"The fucking bastard," I choked.

He hugged me from behind, turning me into his arms.

"What did he do?"

I shook my head, the comfort from his embrace causing the tears to fall. He felt the movement against his shoulder and pulled me tighter. Talk about role-reversal. My little boy was consoling me.

"It's okay, Scott. He didn't say anything I haven't already pointed out to myself."

"About the baby?"

"No. About me being too old for Adam."

I wanted Scott to know what upset me. I didn't want him thinking this was because I was jealous of the impending birth of a child.

Scott's face filled with angry shock. "Like he can talk."

"It's what I said, but it's different for men."

"No, Mum, it's not. I'm gonna kill the prick."

I barely had time to register Scott's words when he set me aside and stormed out of the laundry room.

"DAD!"

I heard Scott scream his father's name. I dashed the tears from my eyes and raced after him. Rob was in the hallway with the front door cracked open, obviously just about to leave.

"What the fuck, Dad? Why is it okay for you to screw a young chick, get her banged up, and then hand out the cigars like you're some fucking hero?" Scott was taller than his father by only a couple of inches, but he was a bigger build, and was now leaning over him, right in his face.

"Scott, calm down." Robert spoke the words in a deadly quiet voice, holding his own anger in check.

"NO. I won't fucking calm down." He put his palm onto the open door and pushed hard until it closed, cutting off his father's escape route. "Mum has every right ... every fucking right to happiness, just as much as you do. Did she complain when you decided you didn't want to stay married anymore? Did she call your girlfriend names?"

"I would advise you to be very careful about what you say here, Scott," Rob warned.

"Or what?"

"Scott, please," I said in an effort to calm the situation.

Scott had Rob baled up against the front door. One arm on the door frame, above his father's head, the other on his hip, his hand curled into a fist.

I put my hand gently on the arm against his hip. "Let it go." My voice was soft with persuasion.

He didn't look at me, his heated gaze glued to his father's face. I'd never seen him so angry before and I had to admit, I felt a bit frightened.

Just when I was trying to defuse the situation, Robert had to be a dickhead and say the one thing sure to provoke his son.

"Faith." He turned his gaze to me. "Is this the way

you're bringing up our son? Great parenting skills."
Sarcasm dripped from his words as he slowly clapped
his hands.

"That's it!" Scott barked.

With a burst of energy which made me jump back in
fear, Scott pulled his arm from the door and pushed it
up under Rob's neck, easily pinning him against the
wood with superior strength. "You're an asshole. You've
always been a fucking prick. We don't give a shit what
you do. Marry the fake bitch. Have as many babies as
you fucking want and buy your way into your
promotion. But don't you ever fucking come here and
treat Mum like shit, or you will know 'or what'."

I stood back watching the scene before me unfold
with a sense of shock. My hands were held to my mouth
in utter amazement at Scott's aggressive stance against
his dad.

Robs face was red with fury. His blue eyes wide and
looking crazy. His thin sandy hair was messed and lay
flopping around his face.

"Have you gone mad? You're going to regret this,
Scott." His words were bitten out through clenched
teeth.

Scott released his hold on his father and reaching
around him, pulled open the door, forcing his dad to
move. With one arm on Rob's shoulder he shoved him
out the front door. "Yeah, I am mad. Maybe I'll regret
it, but right now - I want you gone."

I watched mesmerized as he slammed the door on
his father and leaned on it with both palms flat, bracing
himself against it, his head bowed. Breathing rapidly,
he strove to calm himself.

I didn't know what to do. Standing frozen to the

spot, my hands still covered my mouth in a combination of awe and distress. A part of me wanted to cheer, the big part. Another part wanted to rush to my baby's side and comfort him.

Only a few months off his eighteenth birthday, my little guy was turning into quite a man.

"Scott?" I spoke the words tentatively, cautious.

My son twisted around, leaning his back against the closed door, his head thrown back against the wood, eyes closed. I could only stare at him, lost for words.

Suddenly a soft chuckle came from him. "Did you see his fucking face?"

Relief washed through me. I didn't realize I had been holding my breath, but I let it out in a whoosh.

His eyes popped open, and they were filled with humour and something else … was it satisfaction?

"Scott?" I moved and went to him.

He pulled me into his arms and hugged me tight. "Sorry, Mum, but the motherfucker had it coming."

"He did?" I pulled a fraction away to look up into his face.

"Hell yeah. He's been badmouthing you and Adam for months now. I've had enough."

"I didn't know he was saying stuff to you. You should have told me."

Scott pulled away and went into the kitchen and I followed. He opened the fridge and pulled out a beer, holding one up for me. I shook my head. He popped the top and took a huge swallow before answering me. Technically, he was too young to drink legally, but there was no way I would stop him.

"I didn't want to upset you. Plus, I thought he would stop after a while."

I didn't want to defend Rob. It was the last thing I wanted to do, but I had to be honest with Scott. "What he said is true, Scott. He's getting applauded and labelled a stud for being with a younger woman and I'm getting classed as a desperate cougar."

He nodded at my words. "That's fucked up. Just ignore them Mum. It's jealousy."

I hugged him and kissed him on his cheek. It was so easy for Scott to explain and brush off. But the real-life problems Rob pointed out were a sore point with me. I knew it was jealousy motivating Rob's and other people's comments, but it didn't mean it hurt any less.

"Thanks, sweetheart. How did I have such a great kid?" I grinned at him, moving away.

"Great parenting skills, I guess," he answered with a wide grin.

I chuckled at his choice of words.

"What's with the going all Hulk on me? You really scared me."

He threw his head back and laughed. "Not as much as I scared the old man."

I joined in. "Omigod, every time I want a good laugh from now on, I'm gonna picture his face." I imitated 'The Hulk.' "You don't want to make me mad... Hulk smash."

Scott guffawed. "Oh, Mum, The Hulk doesn't have an Arnold Schwarzenegger accent ... Get to the choppa."

By this stage we were both laughing hysterically, a belated reaction from the tense standoff. Scott came over, throwing an arm across my shoulders. "Come on, I'll hang out the washing and you go get ready. I'll take you out for dinner, my shout. Just the two of us."

He grinned boyishly, his fly-away hair flopping over

his face. I was charmed by his cuteness overload.

"Okay," I grinned. "I better jump at this opportunity. It's not every day I get to go out on a date with my son who's strangely cashed up. What about the wheels for your car?"

"Where do you think your dinner money is coming from? It's Dad's," he snickered. "I reckon he owes us. Plus, he took off running scared. He's probably forgotten I have the cash he gave me."

18

Adam

Since coming back to Townsville to live, my mother had invited me over for Sunday roasts a few times, knowing it was my favourite. No one did a roast quite like your mum.

I'd worked this weekend on a difficult problem we had been struggling with for months. The owner of an industrial site was organising the building of offices and a workshop for a private waste collection service company. They were having complications with zoning and engineering approval. What had originally seemed a straightforward job had grown into a massive headache - my headache.

Faith had spent the day with Rachel, and after dinner I was going to spend the night at her place for a change. After her run-in ... or rather Scott's run-in with Rob last weekend, her son had taken me aside and made me promise to look out for her.

As if he would even need to say those words to me.

Scott did a brilliant job of playing white knight, but I wish I'd been there. I would've loved an excuse to knock her ex-husband into tomorrow. Although he probably wouldn't have said a thing with me around. Like all cowards, he waited till Faith was on her own. He didn't count on Scott though. I chuckled to myself. I don't think he'll be pulling that stunt again.

I frowned as my thoughts turned to Faith. Something was bothering her. I could see it in her eyes, even though she always made sure she was happy and smiling when we were together. Right from the start, even before embarking on this relationship, I always knew the biggest obstacle I had to overcome was Faith. She had brainwashed herself into believing we were brother and sister, and our sexual hook-ups were somehow wrong, that we were indulging in some incestuous exchange.

Hell, if it was wrong ... bring it on I say.

I chuckled at the thought.

The visit to her mum and dad hadn't helped. Jean and Jonah always pissed me off. It bothered me even more how she always accepted and defended those pathetic excuses for parents. Faith had done it her whole life and was continuing to repeat the pattern. The only good thing about her family was they lived in Tasmania. Too far away to cause any long-term damage.

Jean had upset Faith with her unfiltered and thoughtless words. I could see her demeanour change almost immediately. Nothing I'd said to her since we'd returned had managed to reassure her. My mother was just as bad, and she claimed to love Faith like she was her own daughter. I laugh-snorted at the thought.

"What's so funny dear?" My mum's voice intruded on my thoughts. Without waiting for me to answer, she spoke again. "I can't wait until you produce grandchildren for me, Adam."

Her words made my head pop up from behind the newspaper I was reading at the breakfast bar. I needed to side-track her. "Mmm, something smells awesome Mum. I'm starving. I really missed your Sunday roasts."

"Don't change the subject, dear." She was looking at me over the top of her glasses, her greying blonde hair cut short around her head and longer at the back, brushing her collar and flicking back on the sides. An older version of Rachel, she was in her early sixties, and still attractive, especially her large blue eyes. Eyes that were trained on me now with rapier sharpness.

Not this again.

I sighed and put the paper down on the kitchen counter. "One day maybe."

"How's Faith?" She threw the question at me in a provoking challenge. I wasn't playing.

"Fine." I watched as she wiped her hands on the tea-towel tucked into the pocket of her floral apron.

"She's lucky she has Scott. She had so much trouble getting pregnant, poor thing. Rachel tells me she can't have any more babies."

My mother's words caused a slow burning anger to build in my chest. "So?"

"I'm just saying." She turned to the stove and added the onion she had sliced to the gravy. "I know you've been seeing her a fair bit since you came home."

I glared at her back. "I repeat, so?" I knew where she was going with this, but I wanted her to say the words.

My mum turned back around and looked me in the eyes, a sympathetic look on her face. "So, I know how smitten you were with her as a teen, and I know something happened between you two. And I fully agreed with her response. Faith was a married woman, Adam. Her loyalty was to her husband and her child."

I looked away from her assessing gaze. "But she's not married anymore."

Monique, who had been watching TV in the adjoining family room, sauntered into the kitchen and plonked herself down in the chair next to mine; no doubt she'd been listening into the conversation and now wanted to have her two cents' worth.

My mum leaned across the bench and put her soft hand over mine. My eyes were drawn to the pale coral polish on her small fingernails. "I may not know what took place, but I know she hurt you and drove you away. I only hope you realise any future with Faith is a future without children of your own."

My eyes burned into her. I pulled my hand out from under hers and stood. "Exactly. You don't know what took place. It was me who left of my own volition. It was my choice. And it's my choice to return now."

"I know what happened," Monique piped up.

I turned deadly eyes to her. I took in her dark purple tank top and black yoga pants. Her hair had been straightened and hung in long silky strands, which brushed the countertop she was slouching over. Her face held a know-it-all smirk.

"What?"

She pretended to be surprised by my narrow-eyed look and ignored my glare for her to butt out.

"People at the party told me what happened. I'm sorry I missed the scene," she smirked.

"There wasn't a scene," I snapped.

She twirled a strand of her long black hair around her finger. "That's not what your girlfriend Sandra said."

I snorted, dismissing her comment.

My mother tried to calm the situation. She could see I was getting annoyed. "Monique, it doesn't matter what happened. The important thing is Adam is back here now."

"Yeah, but for how long? Until she drives him away again?" she questioned, an ugly twist to her mouth.

I seriously wanted to slap the smug, snarky, look off her face. She had never liked Faith. Was always jealous of the relationship between Faith, Rachel and me. We didn't leave her out on purpose, it was something that happened unconsciously. But now, I was glad she wasn't a part of our group. Her jealous, foul personality would have caused problems.

I turned on my heel to stalk out of the kitchen before I carried out the very real physical threat running through my head but was stopped by my mum's words. "Adam, you don't understand. I love Faith like she's my own daughter. We all do. But the truth of the matter is, you need to find someone closer to your own age."

"I could hook you up, Adam. You remember my friend, Angela Jackson? You went out with her on a date a couple years ago," Monique suggested.

My sister just couldn't keep her mouth shut.

"Yeah, I remember your friend. Beautiful and boring. Incessantly talking about herself, kinda like you. I've never yawned so much on a date." My tone was snide, but it shut her up. This time I turned and made my way out of the room.

"Adam, wait. We only want you to find someone who can give you children." Mum's voice was pleading and stopped me in my tracks.

I stood in the doorway to the family room, my back stiff with anger. "Don't you mean someone who can give you grandchildren?" I knew it was a low blow, but I couldn't help myself.

At her sharp gasp, I took a deep, calming breath and swivelled around, walking slowly back to my mother and Monique.

With my hands braced on the counter edge, I leaned closer to her face. "Just so we're on the same page, Mum. I came back for Faith. Not for someone younger, and certainly not so I can reproduce." I swung my head around to Monique. "And, I don't 'need' to find anyone else, my age or otherwise. Especially one of your dull friends."

I stood up straight and faced my mother once more. "I'm sorry you can't love Faith unconditionally the way you would your *own daughter* as you claim. But there you have it."

With those words bitten out, I turned on my heel and slammed out of the house, leaving my mother standing open-mouthed in the kitchen.

19

Adam

"**Y**ou're so sneaky." Faith grinned at me as we boarded the seaplane to go across to Hayman Island. I surprised her with a four-day break for us. I knew she'd been feeling down and wanted to cheer her, secretly arranging with her co-worker, Cat, to look after her shop while we went away.

"Are you sure I can't give you some money toward this?" She turned a knit brow toward me.

I rolled my eyes at her. You would think she would be happy to discover I was independently wealthy. Most women would be over-the-moon. Not my Faith. She scowled when I gave her the details of my inheritance, mumbling to herself I was 'out of her league', whatever the fuck that meant.

186

"Ever been in a seaplane before?" I asked as we settled into our seats and buckled the belts over our laps.

"Never." She threw a wide-eyed, happy look my way. "I'm feeling a bit nervous to be honest." Leaning over she whispered to me. "Are you sure this thing is safe?"

"Perfectly." I took her hand in mine.

After picking Faith up at four in the morning and telling her to pack for a few days, we drove from Townsville to Proserpine airport. Four hours later, we were climbing onto the jaunty aircraft.

Hayman Island was one of many in the Whitsunday Group. Only four kilometres long and three kilometres wide and surrounded by sparkling, gem-like waters, it nevertheless had plenty of appeal. I had booked us into one of the luxury penthouse suites and wanted to spend the next few days relaxing under the palm trees, sipping cocktails and swimming in the spacious pools or snorkelling the idyllic crystal waters and reefs.

Mostly I just wanted to spend time with Faith, without family or friends offering well-meaning, but unintentionally cruel relationship advice.

Like our mothers!

My mum had phoned and apologised that very night, but it still rankled she wasn't welcoming Faith with open arms as I'd hoped and expected.

I also needed the break from work. I'd put in long hours over one project, which had finally passed all the approval stages and was now ready for the builders to do their thing.

Following the brief but bumpy flight, we settled into our opulent room and headed down to the poolside restaurant for a late breakfast. With a plateful of tropical fruits, I headed back to our table.

"Do you want to chill by the pool this afternoon? I think I saw a couple of loungers under the palm trees with our names on it."

I picked up a fresh slice of the sweetest mango and fed a piece to Faith. She took a bite, and I popped the remainder into my mouth.

"Oh, my God. Why can't we buy mangoes like this in the supermarket?" she complained, a trickle of juice sliding out the corner of her mouth. Licking it up she grinned. "Sorry, but you knew about my eating disorder before you invited me."

"I know you make a mess, and if we weren't so public, I would have licked it up myself." I threw her a devilish grin.

She looked at me with a doubtful expression. "Oh, really? That's never stopped you before."

The next few days went by exactly how I'd wished them to. We slept in every morning, lazing in bed, making sleepy love until our tummies growled in hunger and we went down to a sumptuous breakfast. Then we'd participated in some activities the resort provided, sailing or sea kayaking, even attempting to stand-up paddle board. Afternoons were spent by the pool reading a book or in the ocean, snorkelling until sunset.

After a late dinner, we strolled hand in hand along the beach or had drinks and danced in one of the wine bars.

It was perfect. But I knew it was too good to be true. Things were running too smoothly.

Enjoying a night-cap, the evening before our last day on the island, we had ensconced ourselves in a large wicker-cane double chair, almost the size of a daybed, discussing plans to retire to our suite and make use of the luxury spa-bath which overlooked the ocean. Leaning on the bar to ask for a bottle of Faith's favourite wine to take up to our room, a voice I'd hoped to never hear again intruded on my thoughts.

"Adam?" A sultry purr came from behind me. "I thought it was you."

Keeley Daniels was a model from Perth who I'd dated some years ago. As I turned from the bar, she enveloped me in a full-body hug before planting a kiss on my surprised lips.

I extracted myself and looked over her head at Faith. Looking small in the huge chair, she rolled her eyes at me.

Keeley followed my gaze. Noticing Faith, she turned, flicking her long brown hair over her shoulder, as though dismissing her as competition and gave me another hug, this time pushing her leg between both of mine.

Fortunately, the barman came with my wine and I pushed her away with firm hands as I took the bottle and arranged to charge it to the room.

"It's been so long, Addy," she pouted her juicy red lips.

She did the 'baby talk' thing I hated so much. Why women thought it was cute was beyond me. I gritted my teeth. I also didn't remember her lips being so full. Maybe some filler to nudge her career along?

"Keeley. Good to see you." I forced myself to smile at her and her two female companions, more stunning models.

"Even better to see you, Addy." Taking a step toward

me, she attempted to push her body into me again, but I had anticipated it and leaned away. Her dark brown eyes flashed with anger.

"We should have a drink for old times' sake. What do you say, girls?" She tried to entice me into complying by including the other girls.

As if.

I kept myself out of her reach. "My girl's waiting for me. Have fun, ladies." I raised the bottle at the trio in farewell.

I side-stepped her, placing a barstool between us and headed back to my seat and Faith, who was now standing and waiting to go to our room.

"Who is she?" Her gaze slid past to the girls I'd left at the bar.

"I want to say 'nobody,' but I know you won't let me get away with that, so ..." I noticed Keeley making her way toward us and sighed loudly. "Let's get out of here before she comes over. I'll explain on the way to our room."

With one hand holding the bottle, I slid my arm around Faith's shoulders and pulled her with me out of the bar.

Faith looked expectantly up at me. "An ex-girlfriend?"

I nodded. "From Perth. Annoying as fuck. We went out, two months tops."

"Did you dump her?" Her gaze held no jealousy, only curiosity.

"I broke up with her," I rephrased her choice of word. "I broke up with all of them."

"All?" Faith's eyes grew round.

I pushed my finger on the elevator button with the

hand holding the bottle, never removing my arm from her body, and now wrapped both arms around her pulling her tighter to me as we waited for our ride. I brushed my chin on her brow and bent to nuzzle the top of her head breathing in her fragrance.

"Uni and my band. Then Europe and building my career," I said, and shrugged. "I didn't have time."

How could I confess I only went out with anyone for a couple of months at a time? And only then, when I was absolutely driven by nature's hormones. None of them were Faith. I couldn't tell her. It would give away too much. She wasn't ready yet.

***

"What did you forget?"

Faith was rummaging around in her woven bag she'd brought down to the pool.

"My reading glasses. I thought I stuck them in here when I grabbed my book.

I looked over at her. She was wearing one of her many baseball caps she'd brought with her, one for every hour of the day it felt like. She'd pulled her hair up into a ponytail and it now poked out of the hole in the back of the cap. Her sunnies were on the table between our chairs and her book on her lap.

"Oh, I must have left them in the room," her tone sounded irritated. "I'll quickly run up and get them." Sitting, she slipped her feet into black scuffs.

I admired the burnt orange bathing suit she wore. It was a 'James Bond Girl' one-piece sleeveless wetsuit style in snakeskin print. The sides were strips of black material. It was eye-catching and sexy. But the best part: it had a heavy zipper from her chin down to below her navel. Demure, yet enticing with just a slide of a zip.

"No, I'll get them for you." Standing, I pulled on my tank top and pushed my feet into navy thongs. "I'll bring back a couple of menus with me. I'm getting a bit peckish."

"Thanks, babe. They're either on the bedside table or in my handbag." She smiled sweetly and blew me a kiss.

I was tempted to do something corny and catch it, but it was too lame, so I resisted, grinning instead.

I'd stepped out of the elevator and was standing at the door to the suite when I heard the bell ding and the swish of the companion elevator's door open. Looking over my shoulder, I groaned under my breath when I saw it was Keeley. She must have followed me up here.

She feigned surprise. "We meet again."

She was wearing a white silky wrap-thing, which swung open to reveal a miniscule white bikini which barely covered her. White high-heeled sandals brought her to eye level with me.

"Hello, Keeley." I turned my back to the door, not even attempting to open it. If I did, I was certain she would barge her way inside and push herself onto me.

"Now we're alone, let's slip into your suite and have a quickie? Your girlfriend never needs to know." She pressed her breasts to my chest and pushed her hips into mine. Looking deeply into my eyes, Keeley blinked innocently and whispered. "I'm so aroused right now. I can feel my nippies getting hard and my pussy wussy creaming for you, Addy."

Okay, now she was really pissing me off. "Nope. Not

gonna happen." I ground my teeth. She'd boxed me in and trapped me against the door.

My hands, which had been planted on the wood of the door as I flattened myself to it in an effort to get away from her, now lifted to push her away. I'd tried to be nice, to be polite, but some women wouldn't take no for an answer. So, I was ready to be the rude prick and tell her to 'fuck the hell off.' I had just placed them on her shoulders when the elevator bell rang once more, and the doors hissed open to reveal Faith.

Shit!

She took two steps out into the hall before freezing and taking in the scene. My stomach clenched, and my chest turned tight. I wanted to be physically sick.

It must have looked damning. Me standing there with my hands-on Keeley's shoulders and her body pressed suggestively to mine. I threw a combination of a 'help me' and 'I'm sorry' look at Faith.

Tightening her lips, she shook her head and walked the few steps needed to reach us. I was lost for words, completely dumbstruck, wondering how I would get out of this.

Ever the opportunist, Keeley threw her head back and smiled at Faith. A rehearsed sexy pout, as fake as any model's pose. "Oops," she giggled, pressing one long fingernail into her bottom lip in a little girl fashion. "We've been caught."

Faith stood next to me, effectively ignoring Keeley. "I remembered where I left my glasses. Outside, on the table on the balcony. You would never have looked there, so I thought I'd better come up and get them myself." She looked at Keeley then. "Oh, hello," she said.

We stared at Faith dumbfounded.

Faith turned and looked at me, lifting her eyebrows. "Key-card, darling?"

It was in my hand. The hand I still rested on Keeley's shoulders. I handed it to her, still struggling to find my voice.

Taking it from my fingers she looked down at it, then back up at me. "Babe, if I ever get so desperate for a man's attention I would throw myself at him, even though he's made it painfully obvious he's not interested, please kill me. Because it would be just so sad and tragic."

A huge smile stretched across my lips and catching onto her wonderful put-down I chimed in. "But you would never do that, sweetheart, you have too much class to be so lame."

Faith looked over at Keeley, her gaze running up and down the length of her body. "Yeah, good call. It's something only a 'skank' would do."

The 'skank' took a step back, still speechless with shock, a red flush seeping over her face. She'd been outplayed. Faith slid the key-card into the slot and unlocked the door. With a quiet 'snick' it opened.

Twisting the handle, she turned back to Keeley. "If you'll excuse us, we need some privacy."

Faith opened the door, and we both entered our suite, shutting the door on the stunned model standing in the hallway.

Once the door closed, we both burst out laughing.

After a few seconds there was a loud bang on the door and a 'Fuck you!' yelled out, before we heard footsteps clacking on the tiles as she left.

We howled even harder. I scooped Faith up into my

arms and swung her around. "Oh … sweetheart." I said between loud guffaws. "You are priceless. Did you see her face?"

"I know." She chuckled. "She may be beautiful, but she's an idiot."

I threw us both onto the bed and we bounced as we landed, still laughing hysterically. I wiped the tears from my eyes and rolled over, so Faith was under me. I caught her lips with mine.

"She's not beautiful. You are," I stated, kissing her again. "And clever. And naughty. And sexy." I dropped a quick kiss on her mouth with each compliment I delivered. The relief I felt washing over me was euphoric.

When Faith stepped out of the elevator, my world heaved and tilted on its axis. I'd never known fear to hit me so hard. In that moment, I believed it was all over and I'd lost her. As if in slow motion, I felt myself unravel at the thought.

"I am pretty clever." Faith smiled widely at me. "I can't wait to tell Rachel. This will go down as the best 'burn' in history. The student has now become the master." She fist-pumped the air.

I held her head between my hands. I'm sure I was gazing at her with love overflowing from my eyes and a stupid, goofy grin on my face. I couldn't help it. I ached to tell her I loved her.

Instead, I did the next best thing. Grabbing hold of the zipper on the front of her bathing suit to slide down, I showed her.

***

"Hey poo-head, time for a shower."

I woke up, a smile twisting my lips before my eyes even opened. Faith had called me that when I was being a jerk as a kid.

I cracked an eye open. She was lying on her side next to me, her head propped on her bent arm. The sheet covered her delectable curves from my view but conveniently, I was sprawled spreadeagled on my back, completely nude.

"Were you ogling me while I was unconscious?" My morning voice sounded croaky.

Faith smiled wickedly. "Still am." Her gaze slid down my body.

I lifted my head off the pillow and looked down. My cock was hard with a morning glory. I chuckled and started to pull the sheet from her body. She held on tight.

"Oh no, buddy. We have to leave in a couple hours. Have a shower with me." With those words she slid out of the bed and walked naked into the bathroom. I loved her confidence. Hearing the water turn on and her humming, I jumped out of bed and joined her in the spacious double shower.

She had soaped up a wash-puff and was sponging her body. I moved in behind her, using my hands I did the same. Moaning she turned and started to wash me too. We smiled when seeing my morning wood hadn't abated.

Faith got down on her knees and soaping up her hands she washed my cock, rinsing it off and licking it in a slow slide from the base to the tip. Swirling her tongue around the head and pushing it into the little hole at the top, she tasted the tiny drop of pre-cum, which had oozed out. Looking up into my face she eased me into her mouth, sucking gently while cupping my balls with her soapy hand.

"Oh God, Faith."

She increased the pressure with my words and drew me in deeper. I pumped deliberately in and out of her mouth. Pulling off completely she grasped me in her soapy palm and stroked my length, letting the bubbles lubricate with each pull.

"Babe ..." My breath hitched.

Sluicing with water she treated me to the same again until with a groan, I pulled her up and urgently pushed her to the cool tiles. My mouth crushed hers and I lifted her up onto my shaft, my fingers pressing into the softness of her butt cheeks.

Her legs wrapped around my waist, her arms clinging to my shoulders while her back was against the shower wall. I entered her quickly, thrusting in and out, the water cascading over my back and running in rivulets down my legs. The only sounds were the harsh panting of our ragged breaths and the soft wet sounds of the water hitting the tiles in rhythm to our undulating coupling.

Pulling out and unwrapping her legs from around me I supported her while turning her to face the glass shower screen. With hands pressed flat against the glass I took her from behind, my much bigger hands firmly covering hers. My fingers interlocked with hers. I almost lifted her off her feet with my upward motion.

"Oh ..." Faith moaned between pumps. One hand left hers and slid down her water slicked body to rub her clit, the other scooped around to stroke a breast.

Within seconds we were both nearing climax, Faith's

orgasm came only nanoseconds before and set off my own. I groaned loudly with my climax, the sound echoing in the bathroom. Dropping my head to the back of hers, my heart drummed furiously against her back.

"Holy crap," she said. "My legs feel shaky."

I wrapped an arm around her waist for support. Pulling her back against my wet body, I bent and kissed her neck. I turned her around in my arms, pulling her face to mine and promised, "I'm never going to get tired of making love to you." My mouth covered hers in a hungry kiss. I had to bite my tongue to stop myself from telling her how I felt, but I knew soon I would have to. I was getting tired of holding back.

Pulling away she turned in my arms grabbing our toothbrushes and squeezing out an equal measure on both before handing mine to me.

"I'm fad we hafe to go home today." Her garbled words, spoken around the toothbrush she'd shoved into her mouth, mirrored my own feelings. I was sad as well.

In actual fact, I dreaded the thought of returning to normality after the idyllic time we'd had together, but I was also excited. Last night I'd decided to step up to the next level in our relationship.

20

Faith

I looked across the crowded reception in an effort to locate Adam. We were at the wedding of his old mate from school, Cheese, Brett Colby. I knew him from years ago too. He was the comedian of Adam's group, always pranking his buddies. I'd copped it on more than one occasion myself. But he was harmless, and one of the few mates Adam had kept in constant contact with over the years.

My gaze found him on the other side of the room. Adam looked exceptionally handsome tonight in a pale mauve, long-sleeved shirt, the sleeves rolled to below his elbows, a black tie at his throat. Black slim-line dress pants caressed his cute butt and tapered down to black shoes. On another man the colour might look too effeminate. On Adam, it just made him look even more delicious, the loose shirt hinting at the muscular chest and strong arms beneath.

I frowned. The woman talking to Adam was stunning. They always seemed to gravitate to him. A bottle redhead, she lacked the pale skin and freckles which plagued the natural ones, with artfully curled tresses falling past her shoulder blades. I couldn't see her eye colour from here, but it was probably something hideous like jade or turquoise.

She was slim in a sexy black figure-hugging dress, and I felt disturbed by the way her hand found excuses to keep touching Adam as they chatted.

His gaze captured mine. He smiled reassurance at me over her head while still listening to the woman's avid conversation.

I groaned inwardly. I guess this was something I would have to get used to and learn to deal with if I was planning on having a life with him. After the run-in with his man-eating ex at Hayman Island two weeks ago, I was growing a thick skin when it came to these forthright females.

The woman before me, on the other hand, was one of my customers, Jocelyn Pemberton. A woman who talked too much about everything and nothing. It was just my bad luck to be ambushed by her. Every time I took a step, in reverse, to try to extract myself, Jocelyn took a step forward, until I was cornered against the table holding the wedding cake. Short of crawling under it to escape, I was trapped.

"Babe, they're playing our song."

Adam, thank god.

He reached around the woman, pulling my hand into

his.

"Excuse us, please." He turned his megawatt smile onto the woman I was imprisoned by. "Faith promised if this song came on, she would dance with me."

The poor woman, she didn't know what hit her. Her mouth grew wide as she beamed back.

And did I see her bat her eyelashes at him?

"You owe me big time," he whispered as he pulled me into his arms.

"Since when has Tiny Dancer been our song?" I jokingly complained, loving his silly sense of humour.

"Every song is our song when I want to dance with you. Didn't you get the memo?"

I chuckled as he pulled me closer and started to sing into my ear. Adam loved to sing. He had a great voice, unlike mine, which sucked. But it didn't stop me from joining in with hushed tones.

He pulled back. "Sweetheart ..." Giving me a tortured expression and twisting a finger in his ear as if to ease the pain, he grinned.

"Get lost," I giggled, lightly punching his shoulder. "I'm not that bad."

"You're not that good either, which makes it all the funnier. You should stick to what you do best."

I looked up at him in query. "Dance?" I joked, knowing perfectly well where this was going.

He pressed his hips into mine in answer. "Yeah, the horizontal type."

Rolling my eyes, I changed the subject. "You look exceptionally handsome tonight," I complimented. "Especially in a tie. Very formal."

"You've seen me in a tie before."

I shook my head. "Nope."

"At my grandmother's funeral."

My mind slipped back to the service. "What ... when you were twelve?"

"Sure. And you told me I looked handsome then, too."

A bubble of laughter escaped from my lips. "That was little boy handsome. This is sexy, women-can't-keep-their-hands-off-you handsome. There's a difference," I informed him. "Speaking of women who can't keep their hands off you ..." I let the sentence hang, but he knew who I meant.

His expression turned grumpy. "Monique set me up on a date a couple years ago on one of my trips home." He was dismissive. "Forget about her. I already have."

I was more than happy to do as he asked, especially when he smiled at me the way he was now.

"There's only one woman whose hands I want on me." He waggled his eyebrows at me. "And who I want my hands on."

I loved the fact Adam couldn't keep his hands off me. Running them from my waist up the back of my dark blue silky dress, he pressed me tighter into his body. The skirt was straight fitting and had multi-layers, the top sat snug, with small capped sleeves. The material of the bodice almost transparent. Its opaque cloth allowing glimpses of the blue bra beneath, showing off the narrowness of my back and moulding my breasts in the front. The neckline was low, but not indecently so. I chose this dress with Adam in mind and I wasn't disappointed.

"You look sexy in this dress. I can't wait to get you home and peel it off." He whispered the words in my ear, they came out husky with need. A hand slid down to my butt and pressed me against his lower body. I felt the hardness between his legs. I pulled back, my eyes flying to his face in surprise. He threw a sheepish smile at me, entirely unrepentant. "I did say you look sexy," he justified.

"Your mum and dad are only a few tables away." I looked around anxiously.

"Don't worry. There's too many people on the dance floor for them to notice us." Adam had manoeuvred us into a dark corner.

We danced for a few songs, a good mix of slow and up-tempo classics. I was having a wonderful night but was thirsty and my shoes were biting into me.

"Want to get a drink?" I motioned with my hand over the loud beat of the music.

He nodded and led me out to the bar area. As we were leaving, the faux redhead from earlier grabbed his forearm. Her ruby nails stood out against his tanned arm. "How about a dance, Adam?"

I was surprised at her brazen hold, considering Adam had made it obvious he had a date for the night.

Adam looked right through her, dismissing her. "Nope. I gotta take a piss," he said, before putting an arm around me and leading me toward the bar.

Ouch. Someone call the fire brigade, cos that girl just got burned.

While Adam ordered our drinks, I casually looked at the redhead hovering at the edge of the dance floor. She was with a group of girls. They tossed filthy looks at me. I looked away, but I couldn't stop the sly smile snaking across my lips.

***

The wedding reception was almost over. It had been an enjoyable night, and I felt so proud to be with Adam. I'd concluded a while ago I was in love with him, and had decided tonight, I'd confess my love. Then make mad, passionate love to my man.

I smiled at my wicked thoughts, gazing around the reception room as many of the guests said their goodbyes and prepared to leave. I felt pleased with the resolution I had made and looked forward to the night ahead when I had Adam alone.

"Hi, Faith."

"Oh, Monique. How are you, sweetheart?" I got up and hugged Adam's sister. "Did you just get here?"

"Yeah, I had another wedding to go to, believe it or not? I wasn't going to come but thought I would stop in to congratulate Cheese," she said.

Her face, so like Adam's, scrunched up searching the room. "Where is he?"

Where Adam had blue eyes, hers were a deep brown, and she was much smaller as well, taking after Rachel's mum.

"He'll be back soon," I said. "He's carrying some gifts out to the car for Cheese."

"And Rachel? I thought for sure she'd be here. Don't tell me she's left already?" Monique asked, her eyes darting around.

"The girls both have gastro, so she's at home." I picked up my glass and drained it, knowing we would be leaving soon as well.

She nodded at my words then looked me over. "So, you two are a couple now?"

I grinned. "I know, unbelievable, huh?"

"Very ... since he was going out with one of my friends not long ago, and no doubt would have asked her to marry him. He came back to Townsville for her." Monique looked around the room. "You must have seen her. She's a gorgeous redhead, Angela Jackson."

Ahh, that explains it.

"He ... he never said anything to me."

Monique sent a scathing look my way. "Why would he? He probably wants to get you out of his system. After all, you're the one who got away."

I looked at her, stunned. "Adam would never do that to me." I was certain of it.

"Maybe, maybe not. You don't know what he's like anymore." She shrugged, dismissive. "But regardless, you're too old for him. I don't understand why you old chicks always want a young guy. Must be a midlife crisis thing," she scoffed.

She might as well have punched me in the gut. I wanted to double over with the pain of it. I could only stare at her.

Why the hell would she say this?

Adam's mum, Julie, returned to the table then, hugging her daughter. "Oh Mon, you shouldn't have bothered coming. The wedding is almost over. The bride and groom are getting ready to leave." She gave her a kiss on the cheek.

I sat in my chair and watched this exchange mutely. My mind filled with painful, chaotic thoughts.

Monique glanced at me over her shoulder, then turned to her mother. "I was just explaining to Faith how we think it's not fair on Adam, now they're together. Poor Ads, he'll never have the opportunity to have children of his own if you two get serious."

I looked at Julie, my eyes feverish in their search of her face, trying to confirm if Monique spoke the truth and hoping to find a friendly ally.

My stomach dropped, and I felt a catch in my breath when I saw the concerned blue eyes, so like Rachel's, turn to me apologetically. "He deserves to have children of his own, dear. Although in all fairness, as he has pointed out to me, it's his decision."

"But ... He ... I'm sure he loves me," I spoke in a tortured rasp. "And I love him."

My eyes shifted between Julie's pitying gaze and Monique's I-told-you-so smugness.

"You're sure he loves you? But he hasn't told you yet, has he?" Monique was quick to jump onto my uncertain statement. "Adam won't break with you. He has something to prove with you," she stated with authority. "It's up to you to do the right thing, Faith. For Adam's sake. If you love him as you claim, that is."

I didn't want to talk to them. I felt my throat close over with a tightness. "I see," I bit out. "I wish you'd mentioned something sooner."

Before I fell so deeply in love.

I looked down at my hands on the table and at the white serviette they were wringing, while I felt like my heart was cracking. Lifting my head, I ran my eyes over the two women who I had always thought of as my own family. They both stared at me expectantly.

What did they want? Were they waiting for me to make some sort of promise to break with Adam?

Their figures blurred out of focus. I felt the hot burn of tears in my eyes and couldn't form a coherent sentence if my life depended on it.

"Excuse me." I stood up and grabbing my purse,

practically ran to the ladies' room and locked myself into a stall.

It never crossed my mind Adam would do that to me. No. I was confident he'd never treat me like a conquest. The love in his eyes proved it.

But the words I'd heard for the past few months rang true. My mother, then Rachel, Rob, and now Monique and Julie, all the people who were closest to me. Adam did deserve better. Someone who could give him the things I couldn't.

I struggled to hold it together, forcing myself to think of other things so I wouldn't cry. It was no use. I felt like every part of me was coming undone. I was like a loose thread, that once tugged, unravelled until the whole garment lay lying like a tangled heap on the ground.

Reeling off some toilet paper, I swiped at my eyes. I wasn't wearing waterproof mascara today and it would be obvious I'd been bawling. Everyone would look at me with pity. Or worse, I'd be a laughingstock.

I stayed in the bathroom as long as I could in an attempt to regain my composure. I heard the loud squeal of the bathroom door opening, and Adam's voice outside my stall. 'Faith? Are you feeling sick?"

Poor love, his voice sounded upset.

I had no idea how I managed to pull myself together enough to call out in a near-normal voice. "I'll be out in a minute."

"Okay, I'll wait in the hall." He stood outside my cubicle for half a minute. Probably wrestling with indecision as to whether my words rang true. Eventually, I heard the door close.

Leaving the stall, I stared at myself in the mirror. I

didn't look shattered. But I sure as hell felt it. Wetting a paper towel, I patted my face and wiped away my panda eyes. Taking out my little cosmetic bag I always carried, I freshened up my makeup and reapplied a few strokes of mascara before stepping out of the bathroom, praying everyone had left.

The hallway was quiet. The only noise, the loud squealing of the door as I exited the powder room. Adam was sitting on a leather chair in the lobby of the hotel and pounced as soon as I stepped out. It was almost deserted. I glanced at the clock on the wall above the front counter. It was after midnight.

"Are you okay?" he asked, concern etched his brow, and he put an arm around my shoulders.

"I'm fine. Just feeling a little sick. Too much champagne." I sent a weak smile in his direction. "Is everyone gone?" I looked past him to the double glass doors, which led into the function room the Colby Wedding had been held in, mentally crossing my fingers the Warner family had left.

"A few stragglers. I gave your regards to Cheese." His scrutiny was intense, and I had to work hard to maintain my poise. "Shall we go?"

I nodded. "Did ... did Monique catch up with you?" I struggled not to allow my hurt at his younger sibling's words show.

"Yes." He moved his arm to my waist and led me out to the parking lot, saying nothing more about her.

The drive home was completed in silence, both lost in our own thoughts. Adam massaged my shoulders in the short ride up in the elevator from the underground car park. "Are you feeling sick still?"

"Uh uh," I murmured. I wanted to act normally, but I

couldn't seem to do it. My heart was crumbling into a million pieces.

"Are you tired?"

"Yes, a little."

"Let me run a nice warm bath for you," Adam offered.

I smiled slightly, shaking my head.

God, he's so sweet. How am I ever going to leave him?

Because I had decided on the drive home, I would bow to convention and release him. Give him up to the life he deserved. The young girls, the wrinkle-free faces and vibrant coloured hair, the energy and ambition of youth, but most of all, to the unborn children. The babies he deserved to have. The babies I could never give him.

When I came out of the en-suite ten minutes later, I found Adam standing on the balcony off the bedroom, a tumbler of amber liquid held tightly in his hand. He was still dressed in his wedding clothes as was I, only I was minus my high heels. I'd brushed my teeth and given myself a good dressing-down in the mirror. I'd always expected this new sexual relationship with Adam to be a temporary thing, and at the back of my mind, if I was being totally honest with myself, I also reluctantly acknowledged he was too good for me.

Tonight, I decided, would be the last hurrah, and in the morning, I would tell him I couldn't see him anymore. I had no idea how I would accomplish the harrowing task. Adam would be upset and try to talk me out of it. But somehow, I had to steel my back and remind myself I was doing this for him.

Stepping out onto the balcony I ran a hand down his

back, letting it glide over the silky warmth of his shirt. Setting his glass on the balcony ledge he turned to me, silently taking me in his arms. I sensed he knew something was amiss, but he said nothing.

Burying his face into my hair, he breathed deep. We stood like that for almost a full minute before I pulled away, and taking his hand in mine, wordlessly led him to the bedroom.

The spicy cinnamon fragrance of the scented candle on the tallboy permeated the room. Standing before him at the side of the bed, I loosened his tie and pulled it free, letting it drop onto the soft rug underfoot.

Next, I unbuttoned his shirt with unsteady hands. Within the glow of the room, I slowly parted the silk material while bestowing gentle butterfly kisses on his body as each piece of clothing fell to the floor.

"You're so beautiful," I whispered reverently.

I made love to Adam with all the love I had in me. Injecting tenderness and emotion into each brush of my lips and every caress of my hand, cherishing this man before me. I had been afraid to let him into my heart, but tonight, on our final night together, I allowed myself to admit the truth - he had always been there.

We fell to the bed, our bodies and hearts entwined, minds and souls merging as one conscious. Passion built until we couldn't be gentle anymore, pleasuring each other with a wistful desperation, each of us sending the other a wordless yearning message of love.

With closed eyes, I savoured every touch of my hands over the smooth curves and sharp angles of his muscular body, committing them to memory. My senses relishing the taste and unique essence of him, before looking deeply into his eyes at the point of climax, conveying my heartfelt love.

Afterward, when we were wrapped in each other's arms, our bodies spent, soaking in the sweet afterglow of our lovemaking, Adam whispered hoarsely, his voice raw with emotion. "Fate ... I love you. I don't know what happened tonight. Whatever I said. Whatever I did. I want you to remember that."

His intense gaze held mine, and my heart hurt to hear him blame himself for the distance that he sensed. I ached with the need to return his words of love, but it would be too cruel. To confess my love, only to leave him. I couldn't do it. My eyes filled with tears, and my throat closed.

"Faith?"

Shaking my head, I pressed my passion-softened lips to his mouth. "Shh, Adam. I'm just feeling emotional."

He held himself still. I could see the conflicting emotions play across his face in the semi-darkness. He must have fought and won the urge to say more and instead held me close. I rolled over, pretending to feel tired and feigned sleep. But silent tears coursed down my cheeks, soaking the pillow.

21

Adam

Faith wasn't beside me when I woke. Pushing myself up I squinted at the digital clock on the bedside table – 5:45 a.m. I groaned and lay back down listening for sounds from the bathroom. When a couple of minutes had passed and still no sound, I threw the sheet off and swung my legs over to the side of the bed. I froze in the act of pulling on my jockey shorts. Her dress was not on the floor. Panic hit my chest with a sharp blow.

Racing into the bathroom and then out into the main body of my apartment I saw no signs of her. Her handbag, which she'd placed on the dining table, was gone.

Moving into the kitchen, I grabbed my mobile phone set to charge the previous night on the counter and pressed her number. It went straight to voicemail.

I called again.

Voicemail again.

Starting to text her, I spotted the note, hung on the refrigerator door with a magnet. I ripped it from the fridge sending the small blue pin flying.

Dear Adam,

I wanted to tell you in person, but you would have talked me out of it. So, being the coward I am, I chose instead to write you a note. Woefully inadequate, I know. I'm so sorry.

Things between us have been beautiful. You have been as wonderful as only you can be. But I can't continue with this. With us. I truly tried. I'm struggling to overcome my demons - the age difference for one, and my own pathetic mindset in regard to our relationship. But mostly the fact that you need to be a father, have your own children. Something I can't give you. I don't need to tell you of all the reasons why you deserve someone your age. Someone better.

I wish you all the very, very best for now and always. If you ever find it in your heart to forgive me and when you've moved on and found happiness, as I pray you will, maybe we can be friends again one day.

Please don't try to see me and change my mind. I'm weak, and I know you'll be able to undermine my decision, but what kind of victory will that be?

Faith xx

I gripped the note so hard in my hand it was almost crumpled in two. I couldn't believe what I'd just read.

I read it a second time.

Scrunching the note, I threw it onto the dining table before racing to the bedroom to thrown on track pants and a T-shirt. Shoving my feet into thongs, I grabbed my car keys from the kitchen hook.

Snatching up my mobile phone I tried ringing again. Voicemail.

Fuck.

I started to text her, my hands shaking so badly I had to stop and take a deep calming breath before tapping out.

FAITH I NEED TO TALK TO YOU. YOU CAN'T END THINGS LIKE THIS. WITH A NOTE. I DESERVE BETTER. I WANT TO SEE YOU!

Slamming out of my apartment, taking the steps two at a time down to the garage, I pressed her number and called again as I ran to my car. She must have her phone turned off. It didn't even ring but went directly to her message-bank again.

Gunning the engine, I drove out of the building as the sun was starting to show over the horizon. My heart raced, battering against my chest in painful thumps. A crazy desperation licking through my veins. My mind scrambled to think of reasons that might have brought this on.

What the fuck had happened last night?

Something at the wedding?

My phone buzzed. I pulled over before an intersection, checking the message.

THAT'S EXACTLY MY POINT. YOU DO DESERVE SO MUCH BETTER. PLEASE RESPECT MY WISHES ADAM. I CAN'T SEE YOU. I NEED TO BE ALONE RIGHT NOW.

I bent my head to the steering wheel. I fought the urge to cry at the swelling tide of pain and frustration engulfing me. My heart pounded, and my chest ached.

It was her damned sense of propriety. I was not her brother, and she was not my bloody sister.

No matter how close we had grown up, for God's sake, I had never felt so far removed from feeling brotherly to another woman as I did to Faith.

Swinging my car around on the empty street I headed back to my apartment. I'd give her the space she requested, but I was determined to find out what had happened at the wedding. People don't change that fast.

My eyes narrowed as I relived the final moments of the wedding.

Monique.

***

There was a hesitant knock on the door.

Faith.

I leapt up from the couch where I'd been slouching for the better portion of the day, yanking open the door.

"Wow, where's the fire?"

My sister Rachel stood on the threshold. I looked past her, but she was alone, which in itself was unusual. She usually had her brood, and on the odd occasion, Faith. Unfortunately, not on this occasion.

"I thought you were someone else."

I kissed her on the cheek, inviting her in and offering her a drink. I went to the fridge and stood in front of the open door staring into the bright interior, my eyes skimming over the contents, forgetting what I was even there for.

"Ads." Rachel stood beside me and gave me a small hug. "You sit down. I'll get us a couple of brews."

I could tell by her sympathetic eyes, she knew. "Have you spoken to her, Rach? Is she okay?"

Even now, even though Faith had been the one to break with me, I knew she was hurting. The paper she'd written on was warped with moisture the ink smudged in places. The evidence suggesting she'd been crying when she wrote it. I'd heard her soft tears at night, foolishly thinking I would give her the time she needed, hoping by the morning she would share her feelings and I could allay her fears.

At first, I worried I'd scared her off with my declaration of love. But she must have known how I felt. It must be written all over my face. Noticeable in all my actions toward her, and crystal clear in our lovemaking.

At a young age, Faith had crawled underneath my skin and set up residence in my heart, like a hunger, gnawing at me for years. Until recently, I had never experienced a happiness more intense than the one I felt filling my heart when I was with her.

I would not allow it to end!

"I haven't seen her or spoken with her, Adam." She handed a beer to me. Opening it I took a long swallow before spinning on my heel and flopped back onto the sofa.

"What? Then how do you know? Ah... Monique..."

I called my sister as soon I thought she might be awake. She wasn't. But I didn't give a great flying fuck, driving over and forcing her to answer my questions with her claims of a raging hangover.

"She reckons she was drunk." Rachel weakly defended her half-sister.

"Bull-fucking-shit," I snarled, jumping off the couch. "Come on, Rach, you know she's always been jealous of our relationship with Faith."

She nodded her head in acknowledgment. "I agree, but she still reckons she'd been drinking and spoke before she thought about it. You said some harsh things to her."

I looked at her, my eyes hard. "Worse than what she said to Faith? The lies she told?"

"You called her the C-word," Rachel mumbled.

I looked at her incredulous. "Trust me, if I could've thought of a worse word, I would have used it. I don't want that bitch in my life. Ever!"

"Wow." Rachel opened her eyes wide in shock. "And Mum?"

"I already told Mum how I felt about Faith. She had no right. No fucking business, sticking her nose in." I was worked up now, righteous anger simmering in me.

There was an awkward silence. Rachel was smart enough not to defend them to me in my frame of mind.

I paced around the room, gulping down my beer without consciously realising. "They're my family.

217

They're supposed to love me. Want me to be happy. Instead, they fucking ... ruin everything." I threw my empty bottle at the brick wall with those last two words, smashing it into pieces with the force of my anger. I turned on Rachel, who stood by the dining table, a look of shocked fear on her face.

"I've a good mind to take Faith and move away again."

"Adam, NO!" She put her beer on the table and rushed to my side, grabbing my arm. "I told Mum and Mon they needed to come over and apologise to you."

"Me?" I whisper-yelled in disbelief. "They need to apologise to Faith. And beg her forgiveness." I wrenched my arm from Rachel's grasp. "It doesn't matter now. I don't want to see them. I can't."

"Your dad's so angry, too. He's had no part of this. If you move away, you'll punish him. Don't let others drive you away again."

"Again?" I lifted my head, my eyes burned into Rachel and I raised my voice. "How many times do I fucking need to tell everyone? Faith didn't drive me away. I chose to leave because I was so much in love with her, I couldn't stand to see her with someone else."

"Oh." Rachel mouthed the word so soft it barely came out as a whisper.

There was a long aching silence. Awkward and uncomfortable. Both of us consumed by our own thoughts.

My throat was tight, and my voice came out in a raspy strain. "Go talk to her, Rach. See what she says," I begged my sister.

"I've tried. She has her phone turned off or

something. It keeps going to message bank. I even drove over, but she told Scott to say she didn't want to see anyone right now."

I'd tried calling Scott, too, and had received the same message.

Rachel sighed, walking to the table and taking a swig of her beer. "I don't know what to do either. Maybe give her some time?"

"I can't do it again, Rach." I looked at her, feeling lost. My heart was breaking. The pain of Faith not in my life was like an amputation, my body pumping blood to a part of me which was missing.

"Oh, Ads." Rachel came over to me and took me in her arms.

I let myself be comforted by my big sister. My eyes stinging with unshed tears.

Rachel cursed Faith. "I'm so angry with her right now. It's just as well she's not talking to me. I'd probably say something I'd regret. Can't she see you two are meant to be together?"

I pulled away and gave her a sad smile. "I thought she was starting to. But then Monique had to fuck it all up."

"It's not only Monique." Rachel pulled out a chair at the dining table and sat down, putting some distance between us.

I frowned. "What do you mean? Is there something else I should know?" I joined her at the table, my jaw tightening.

Rachel sighed and looked away before turning back and playing with the balled-up note from Faith, which I had left on the table. I'd been glaring at it all day but was reluctant to throw it out.

"Adam you don't realize how hard it is for a woman with a younger man. People always pointing out the problems she'll face, and not always in a nice way." She looked into my eyes. "Women can be jealous or catty."

"I do know, Rach. Do you think I'm immune?" I pushed my chair back and stood up, running my fingers through my hair. "My mates are always ribbing me about having an older woman as well. I get called 'Hugh Jackman' and, 'what's it like to fuck your mother?' Or here's the classic. I get called her 'toy boy'.

Rachel chewed her lip, biting back a smile. "Hmm, I didn't know. What do you do?"

"I just laugh it off. What else can I do? After so many years of living without Faith in my life, and now... feeling the happiest I've ever been. Hell, it's worth all the shit."

"Have you told Faith?"

"Seriously?" I looked at her disbelievingly. "It would only make her feel worse."

"Oh... right. Well, someone needs to talk to Faith and tell her." Rachel looked sheepish. "The part about you feeling the happiest, that is."

"What do you think I've been trying to do?" I laughed sadly, throwing myself back onto the couch.

"The thing is, Ads, Faith was already suffering from low self-esteem when her marriage broke. Then on top of it all, her dick-head husband gets a much younger wife who is also beautiful, intelligent, and pregnant. Something Faith was unable to do. Everyone seems to be telling her you should be a father. She thinks you deserve to have a family too."

Rachel came to sit next to me on the couch and put her hand over mine, resting on my knee.

"That's ridiculous," I scoffed.

"I'm guilty of it too, Adam. Faith mentioned you deserved to be a dad, and I agreed. I didn't help the situation. Sorry." She looked remorseful.

I stared at her in a mixture of distrust and annoyance. I surged out of the sofa almost kicking over the coffee table in my haste. "Aww fuck, Rach." My hands lifted to my head, and I raked my fingers into my hairs thickness, clasping two handfuls in frustrated anger. "You know how much she values your opinion. And then Mum and Monique said the same thing to her."

She looked down at her hands in her lap and spoke in a hushed tone. "So did her mother, and Rob as well. In fact, none of her family have supported her. Except maybe Scott."

"It's complete crap. I could fall in love with a younger woman, get married and then find out she can't have kids. So, do I divorce her and look for someone who is fertile? 'Excuse me, can you prove you can get pregnant and have a baby before I propose?'" I mocked sarcastically. "I don't even know if I can make a woman pregnant. Maybe I fire blanks."

"Oh hell, Adam, you're right. I'm so sorry. What a lousy friend I am. If it's any consolation, I did tell her it was your choice."

I turned back to her, seeing her distressed face and her watery eyes. I wanted to feel sympathy, but I couldn't. Instead, I swiped her beer off the coffee table and emptied the bottle in one long swallow. "I have to talk to her," I stated emphatically.

"Let me talk to her first," Rachel pleaded. "We'll give her, her space. Allow her to do some soul searching for a couple of days. Then I'll go see her on Wednesday night. I'll pave the way for you, then you can see her on the weekend."

"A whole week?" I started to shake my head negatively.

"Five days." Rachel negotiated. "Let me talk to her? Please Adam. I know how she thinks. Then you can see her on Friday."

She came over and hugged me. "I owe you," she said.

Against my better judgement, I reluctantly agreed with her scheme.

22

Faith

Pulling into my drive, I pressed the button on the automatic garage door, waiting for it to open before driving into the darkened interior. Getting out, I opened the boot and retrieved the four bags of groceries I had picked up on my way home from work. Two bags in each hand, my handbag slung over my shoulder, and my car keys looped around my finger, I squeezed past the junk in my garage to the shoppers-entry door into the house.

"Hey, stranger."

I froze.

Rachel.

I should have known my best friend would corner me in the end. Initially there had been over thirteen missed calls from her, but then silence. I knew better than to believe Rachel had given up and instead acknowledged she was giving me the space I'd requested.

Three days?

More than I had expected.

I looked around for her car. She must have parked around the corner and waited for me.

Sneaky.

"Hey you." I gave a smile filled with sorrow to my friend.

Pressing the button on my central lock, I heard the distinct thud of the car doors locking. I turned toward the house door, juggling my over-sized handbag and unlocked it, entering into the kitchen. I expected Rachel to follow me and wasn't disappointed when she came in and started to unpack the bags I had dumped on the counter.

"Peanut butter cups, huh? That bad?"

My gaze travelled from the four bars of chocolate on the counter then up to her sympathetic expression.

Aww shit.

Tears filled my eyes, and I gave her a watery, wobbly smile. "It gets worse." I heard the cry in my voice as I spoke. "There's two packets of Lollygobble Bliss Bombs and a large tub of Old English Toffee ice-cream."

Rachel made a clucking sound and enclosed me into her arms. The tears flowed like a burst dam and I sobbed loudly. The previous three day's misery had taken their toll. There was only so much a girl could do to keep it all together, and I had reached the end of my shaky, questionable tether.

Yanking myself out of Rachel's arms, I moved to the adjoining family room and tore a handful of tissues out of the box on the corner table. I swiped at my eyes and blew my nose noisily.

"Thanks," I croaked, my voice thick with emotion. "I was holding it together until now."

"You need to talk to someone," she stated, in her matter-of-fact voice.

"I know." I gave a dejected nod.

"I fucking want to kill you, you know," Rachel said in mock anger.

"I want you to kill me," I threw back.

"Faith, you can always talk to me, no matter what." She pulled me around to sit on the sofa, her arm wrapped around my shoulder.

"I couldn't. I ... I ... promised you." I started to cry in between my words; wet, hiccupping sobs. "I wouldn't ... hurt him ... but I did." The last three words were said in a bawl.

"Yes, you did. Now do you want to tell me why?"

"You know why." I took a deep breath and blew my nose again.

"I know all your lame reasons why. You're too old. He's like a brother, blah, blah, blah. He deserves children ...."

"You said it yourself," I cut in.

"I know I did and I'm so sorry. It was a mistake. But I also said it's his decision, if you remember?"

I shook my head and looked down at my hands in my lap, scrunching up the wad of tissues. "What about my decision?" I whispered.

"What's your decision? That you're too weak to fight

for something worth keeping? That you don't want to deal with anyone who says negative things to you? That you can't challenge the social norms?" She fired the words at me like bullets, and I'm not going to pretend they didn't wound. But at this moment, everything hurt, so what were a few more barbs?

I looked at the disappointment in my friend's face. "When you put it like that, it makes me sound weak and pathetic. But you don't know what it's like. People telling me to my face I'm too old, or I'm a desperate cougar. I've got nothing to offer and I'm ruining his life."

Tears started to well again, but I pressed my fingers into my eyes to halt their flow.

"Oh, sweetie, I'm sure it must be awful." Rachel pulled my hands away from my face and held them.

"I spoke with Adam the other day and he claims he gets them, too; jealous people saying mean things to him."

"He does?" I squeaked.

Rachel's voice softened. "You know what he said?"

I shook my head mutely.

"He said it was worth it to be with you."

"Ooh." My lips trembled, and a fresh flow of tears threatened to fall.

"He wants to talk to you, Faith. You know he loves you. And you told me you love him, too."

"It's because I love him," I cried.

"No, it's not. It's because you're scared of failure."

I raised watery eyes to hers and acknowledged her correct assumption. "I can't see him now."

"Why not?"

"I just can't. I need to ... I don't know. I can't think

straight ... I need to process. I don't want to make the mistake I made last time, acting on my emotions and not giving myself time to sort out what I wanted. What I genuinely wanted."

"But that's exactly what you are doing ... Again!" I heard the anger in her voice.

"I don't know what else to do. Everybody seems to blame me and expect me to be the responsible one. I don't want your mum and sister to hate me. I'm barely getting over the last time when they looked at me with disgust. They're family to me Rachel. You know I love them," I pleaded with her to understand why I felt so confused.

"Don't worry about them. Steve's family can't stand me. Do I let it worry me?" Rachel looked into my eyes.

"Yes."

"Okay, true." She pulled a face at me. "But I didn't allow them to break us up. And that's the main thing." I let her words sink in without comment.

"He's not going to let it go, Faith. He's giving you until Friday," she warned.

"Rachel ..." I implored my friend. "Please tell him I don't want to see him. I need time to get my head straight. I can't deal."

"Of course, hon, I'll tell him," Rachel confirmed. "But expect to see him Friday."

23

Faith

I poured myself a glass of white wine and took a small sip, feeling the cool liquid slide down my throat. This was my third glass, and I wasn't feeling the slightest bit tipsy.

Darn it!

The evening yawned ahead of me, dismal and empty. I really should think about what I was going to have for dinner, but my appetite was non-existent. I'd made the effort to cook and eat this past week for Scott's benefit. Although, I would hardly describe pushing my food from one pile to another eating.

Since Scott was away tonight, I hadn't even taken out

any meat from the freezer, and the few times I'd gone into the kitchen today was to pour more wine into my glass. I moped about the house, wandering from room to room, in an aimless drift.

Nothing on TV appealed. I surfed through Netflix but couldn't settle on any show. Picking up a book, I read the same page over and over, before I put it down in defeat. Even music made me feel sad. I couldn't seem to draw my attention away from what was always on my mind.

Adam.

I felt the burn of fresh tears and a lump formed in my throat. I took a sip of my wine in an attempt to flush it down. But it was no use.

"Again?" I said aloud to 'Dude' who had sauntered into the family room. "You would think there were no more tears left?"

The cat jumped onto my lap and I stroked him while he purred loudly. Was Rachel right? Should I talk to him? She said he would give me until Friday. I'd gone out of the house Friday. Like the coward I am.

After work I spent the evening at Cat's house hiding, even to the point of sleeping in her spare room. Cat, although kind enough to let me stay, gave me a firm lecture, shaming me for rejecting him.

But I was so weak.

Scared even.

I loved Adam so much but felt torn. On the one hand, I didn't know how I would go on without him, trying to form some semblance of a normal life.

Then there was the part of me that felt I'd messed up his life already. That I was no good for him and knew he could find better.

Much better.

Should I do the right thing and let him go?

Should I do the right thing and allow us to love each other?

The questions orbited inside my brain like a forgotten satellite.

"Ugh, I don't fucking know," I yelled the words in the hushed room, scaring the cat who jumped off my lap and skittered out of the room.

I knew I was putting off the inevitable. He would probably come by today. But I wasn't ready to see him. My mind still a jumble.

It was evening now, and still no contact. Maybe he had given up?

I hoped so.

LIAR. My conscience screamed at me.

I'm a fucking idiot.

I was the one who broke up with him. I was the one who said I didn't want to see him. I was the one rejecting all his calls and text messages.

I was also the one aching for him.

Clearly, I'm insane.

But it was for his own good.

Or was it?

Oh... I don't know anymore. I'm so confused.

I got up and paced restlessly, finding myself on the back patio. Sitting, I idly sipped on my wine and with one bare foot, rocked myself on the swing seat. After work I'd had a quick shower and changed into denim shorts and a pink tank top. But now what?

I didn't want to go out. Or see anyone for that matter. Hell no. I wasn't good company. Maybe I should get drunk? Rip-roaring drunk. Drown my problems in the sweet release of alcohol. I lifted the glass and downed the remainder of my wine, almost half a glass in one gigantic swallow. I licked my lips and smiled.

"Right. At least I have a plan now." I got up from the chair and made my way into the kitchen. Perfectly steady. "Where's the wine?" I was examining the alcohol percentage on the bottle after emptying the remainder into my glass when there was a knock at the door.

My heart beat faster.

Adam.

I silently raced to look out the front window. I saw Adam's dark dual-cab in my drive. My heart beat double time now.

I went to the locked front door, wineglass in hand. "I can't see you, Adam," I called through the wooden door.

"Faith, enough is enough now. Open this door and talk to me, for fuck's sake." His words were clipped and terse.

"No. Please go away."

"Why won't you talk to me?" he snapped. "You can't end a relationship like this." He sounded enraged. "With words on a piece of paper."

Adam never got angry at me.

"I ... I wanted to tell you in person, but I knew you would change my mind and I ... I," I stammered.

I heard some rustling noises then the scrape of a key in the lock.

Dammit, I forgot he knew where I hid the spare key under a loose paver. I pressed against the door pushing all my weight against it.

"Adam, stop it."

"Like hell I will," he shouted and started to push harder.

The door opened a fraction.

"What's got into you Faith? I've never known you to be like this before." I heard the urgency in his voice and pretended to give in.

"Okay. Okay. Stop pushing on the door."

Once he eased pressure, I slammed it shut the few inches he had pushed it open, locked it again and slid the dead bolt into place this time. Pressing my weight once again against the wood.

"Fuck it, Faith." He banged against the door with his hand and kicked against the wood, causing it to shudder. "Open this door," he yelled, the frustration evident in his voice.

"I can't. Please give me more time," I called out.

"NO. No more time." He kicked at the door and I felt it bounce against my back, and the sharp crack of splintering wood.

I gasped. It only made me push harder in an attempt to keep it locked.

Then suddenly, it was quiet. I listened intently my back pressed against the solid wood. There was not a sound.

I crept from my position and peeked out the window, kneeling on the couch in the front lounge-room to get a better view while pushing the curtains to the side. His vehicle was still in the drive. It was difficult to see in the twilight, to tell if he was in his car or not, and the shrubbery in front of the window blocked my view of the porch outside my front door.

"You know; I couldn't believe it when you said you

wouldn't see me."

I jumped when I heard the tortured voice behind me.

Adam had hurdled the side gate and gone around the back to enter through the patio door I had myself entered only moments before.

I turned from the window. I knew I'd have to face him eventually and resigned myself to it now.

"Why, Faith?" He groaned like he'd been hit in the abdomen.

He looked beautiful even in his disturbed state. My eyes hungrily devoured him standing there in the hallway. He held his body in a rigid line, his jaw uncompromising. Dark circles under his eyes made their colour stand out even more. His rumpled hair and drawn face a testament to the rough week he'd had. Dark blue jeans, taut against his hips, and equally dark blue T-shirt with black joggers completed his outfit. Even now, I couldn't help but be aware of his sexuality.

"You know why, Adam. You would have talked me out of it and second guessed me. And ... and I'm pathetic where you're concerned."

"Because you know they're feeble excuses," he rapped out, furious.

"They're not ... I'm too old for ..."

"Faith," he barked out, cutting me off. I'd never seen Adam like this before. He was so commanding and determined.

"It doesn't matter what reasons you come up with why we can't be together. I've thought of them all, in detail, and discarded every one of them. At the end of the day it's about you and me. I don't care if you have wrinkles or if you have grey hair. I don't care if you put on weight or lose weight. I simply don't care that you're older than me. I love you Faith. I always have."

I sucked in my breath at his words of love, sharp and audible, I was unable to speak. He moved down the hallway until he was standing before me in the living room. I looked up at him from my position on the couch. I had been bent over the back of the sofa, looking out the front window, but now I knelt on the cushions, sitting back on my heels.

"You know you were meant to be with me. Just as I know I was meant to be with you." He raked a hand into his hair. "I've tried living without you. For eleven, long, fucking years. Dating other women ... sleeping with them ... trying to replace you. Wanting to forget you." He paused, his next words whispered, but they came out like a scream of pain. "But I can't."

"Oh."

I was completely shattered by him. The things he said. The way he looked at me in tormented longing. The feelings he evoked.

My eyes once again filled with hot moisture at his words. I closed them briefly, feeling such despair at his pain. Pain I had caused.

"It was all a waste of time, Faith. I couldn't get rid of this empty feeling, here." He raised his right hand and placed it onto his chest. I watched the muscles of his neck as he swallowed with difficulty, noting the pulse ticking rapidly in the strong column. His words made my heart hurt.

Oh, dear lord, but I loved him.

I closed my eyes again as a tide of longing surged through me and threatened to sweep me away. I felt the need to make some token resistance before capitulating completely. I opened my eyes and gazed at his tortured face.

"But what about children?" I asked in a small, uncertain voice.

Adam moved to the couch and knelt before me, so he was eye level. Removing the wineglass from my hand, he gulped down a huge mouthful and put the near-empty vessel on the coffee table behind him. With shaking hands on either side of my head, he looked deeply into my eyes, anxiety etched in his.

"If you want children, we can look at options. But all I want is you." He leaned forward and took my lips in an urgent kiss, groaning softly against my mouth. He pulled away to make this promise to me. "Fate ... I will never, never, love anyone on this planet as much as I love you."

My heart did a crazy flip flop at his words.

I could see the emotion causing moisture to glisten in his eyes and I was overwhelmed at the extent of his love for me. My hand rose involuntarily and cupped his face.

My throat tightened, and my voice thickened with feeling. "I love you, too, Adam. I wanted to tell you ... so many times. But I was scared."

He sucked in a ragged breath at my declaration, his tortured gaze running over my face as though to verify my words. I wiped at the tear which had overflowed and trickled down his hard cheek, pressing my lips to their damp path.

He pulled me tight into his embrace and I felt a shudder shake his frame with his hug. My own eyes started to fill up with tears and I felt them run down my face to splash onto his shoulder.

"Oh, Adam, I've been so foolish. I'm so sorry for

hurting you. I do love you, so much." The sentiment tumbled out of me. "I have for years. The reason I was so furious with you when you kissed me at your party, was because I was turned on. I felt guilty, and scared, and angry ... not at you." I pulled out of his arms to look at him and laugh shakily. "Never at you, sweetheart."

He wiped my wet face with his fingertips.

Now I'd started, the words wouldn't stop flowing from my mouth. "I was angry with myself. Angry I wasn't single, or young, or ..."

As I spoke, he dropped kisses on my lips. "No, you were perfect, Faith."

"God, I wish I was." I could see his eyes roaming my face as I blurted out my confession. "You reduced me to feeling like a teenager, and I was pissed off about that, too. I kept feeling like I was dirty and bad. Like I should have known better."

"Not bad. Badass." Another kiss.

"I was a married woman, Adam. And not only that, but I ... I'd held you as a baby and now, I wanted to hold you as a man. It was wrong."

"So wrong. But so right." The beginnings of a wicked smile curved his lips.

I smiled at his teasing, wrapping my arms around his head and pressed my lips to his in a passionate kiss.

After a few seconds, I drew back and looked deeply into his eyes. "The night of Cheese's wedding, I was going to tell you I loved you. Even though I was afraid of loving you too much and showing you how much I needed you. I was scared you would get over your infatuation with me and move on."

"Never." He chuckled at my words. "You were turned on, huh?" His mouth twisted into a crooked grin.

My mouth dropped open, and I hit him lightly on the chest. "That's what you took away from my confession of love?" I complained in mock outrage.

"I heard other stuff ... dirty ... bad ... I made you feel like a teenager."

I laughed, my heart feeling so light.

Adam kissed me repeatedly with tender, lingering kisses until they turned ravenous and greedy, his tongue slipping between my lips to taste my mouth, pushing me back against the cushions with his need.

He pulled away just as the passion grew intense. His eyes sought mine, a loving, earnest expression in their depths.

"Fate ... I want to marry you. I want you to be mine. And I want to be yours. But I can't be constantly reassuring you of my love, babe. I want you to know I intend to love you forever ... No. Longer. Even forever isn't long enough."

I beamed at him.

He continued. "I will never cheat on you and I will always have your back. I want you to trust me and believe in me. As I will you. Will you marry me, and be mine?"

I watched him hold very still, even now unsure of my answer. "Yes, Adam. Yes, yes, a million times yes. A trillion times yes. I want to marry you. These last few days without you have been hell. I've felt torn apart inside. I didn't want to let you go, but I felt I had to. I can face adversity with you by my side. I know now. I do trust you and believe in you. I don't want my life to just exist. I had a taste this week. I want it to flourish with love. And anyway, I don't even know if I can stand anyone else touching me after you. You've spoiled me for anybody else you know, Mr. Warner."

"Good. A taste of your own medicine then."

Adam pulled me down off the couch until I was straddling his lap. I felt his arousal and wiggled against him, leaning forward pressing my mouth to his.

"I'm not waiting so you can change your mind either," he said against my mouth. "I want to get married in a registry office as soon as I can get the license organised, then later, we can have a big ceremony."

"What? I don't get a say in it?"

"Nope. Do whatever you like with the wedding ceremony, but this I need to do."

EPILOGUE

Adam

I was conscious of the smiles I received as I rode up in the elevator, a plush teddy bear under each arm. Both white, but one had a blue ribbon tied in a bow around its neck, the other a pink one. I'd gone home for a quick shower and a change of clothes before heading back to the hospital after having been there from mid-afternoon the previous day until the early hours of the morning.

Dead tired, but so buoyed up and high on parental love, I couldn't sleep even if I'd wanted to.

Faith.

I couldn't wait to see her again, even though I'd been gone only a few hours. In the past two years we'd been married, we hadn't been separated for a single night, and I was reluctant to do so now.

She was so incredibly happy today when she'd brought our two beautiful babies into the world. Twins - a boy and girl. She said it made her life complete.

I was happy just to have her, my life whole the day I took her as my wife. The babies? Well... they were icing on the cake.

Only the cutest icing.

I swept into the room, a big grin on my face. She was sound asleep, her cheeks flushed. Two transparent Perspex bassinets sat on either side of the bed. One with a small pink card pushed into the holder, the other blue.

I leaned over and looked at the little sleeping bundles making soft sucking noises and a little yawn. I placed a teddy into each baby bed, dropping a kiss on tiny heads wearing miniature white caps over their thick black hair.

Tiptoeing past the cribs, I dropped a gentle butterfly kiss on my wife's brow, not wanting to wake her, the exhausted slumber leaving her pale eyelids closed. Her lashes making small dark semi-circles against the deep mauve under her eyes.

The last few weeks of the pregnancy had taken their toll on her energy levels. We were in fact lucky to have had the babies. With two miscarriages since our marriage, and after almost losing the twins earlier in the pregnancy, Faith had been confined to bed rest during the last trimester.

I'd taken six months off work to stay at home and help out during the difficult pregnancy. With the twins arriving earlier than expected, I was looking forward to helping her nurse, cuddle, and bathe them. It would be an exciting challenge in the next chapter of our lives.

With the help of fertility drugs, Faith had successfully conceived with the twins in the second year of our marriage. I was secretly glad to have her to myself for the first twelve months without the worry of her delicate pregnancy. We'd sold her house and bought a place together. A year later, Scott had moved out with his girlfriend to rent my old apartment.

As if I'd conjured him up, Scott walked into the room, a huge bouquet of white roses in his hand.

"Shh." I lifted a finger to my lips and pointed to the sleeping trio.

He put the flowers on a vacant chair and peered in the cribs. Giving a silent thumb's up he said, "Awesome, Ads."

Looking over at his mother lying asleep in the bed he whispered, "Mum?"

"Exhausted, but all good."

"I gotta go to work," he mouthed.

I got up and walked Scott down the hallway, averse to leaving Faith for too long.

"Good work, mate." Scott thumped me on the back.

I laughed. "Your mum did all the work. You know that, right?"

Scott chuckled. "Yeah, and I'm sure she'll never let us forget it either," he joked. "She's okay? No probs?" Scott asked again, a frown creasing his brow.

"Nah, she's a trooper."

"I'll come back tonight with Jessica," Scott promised. Jessica was his latest girlfriend, and the one who he seemed to be most serious about. "Aunty Rachel isn't coming until after school."

I nodded. "Yeah, she texted me. She promised the girls she'd bring them. Steve's dropping in after work.

I'm glad. Your mum needs to rest."

Scott put a hand up in farewell. As I waved him off, I reflected on the whole family situation. The first few months had been intense with my mother and sister. Even after they had apologised profusely to Faith, the relationship remained somewhat strained - on my side more than Faith's. Hopefully, the arrival of another set of twins would bring a much-needed boost of love.

I snoozed in the chair while Faith, out to the world, slept until the morning shift changed and the new nurses came to check on their patient.

She woke, looked up at me and smiled gently. "Look what we did."

"You did you mean? Fantastic job, babe." I leaned over and kissed her on her forehead while the nurse took her blood pressure before checking on the babies. They both still slept.

Faith looked at the flowers the nurse had picked up to admire.

"Scott dropped by on his way to work. He couldn't stay. He's promised to come back this evening."

She nodded at my words and pulled herself up to sit up in bed.

When the nurse had left, promising to put Scott's flowers into a vase, I moved to the bed and pulled her gently into my arms, careful in case she was sore and uncomfortable.

"Are you happy with their names?" She turned questioning eyes to mine.

Since we couldn't agree on both names, we decided Faith would have the final say on our daughter's name, and I would on our son's.

I nodded, but before I could say more, as if on cue, one of the babies started to stir and let out a little cat-like cry. I stood and bent over the clear crib to scoop our little girl up. "Good morning, Presley Paige Warner. Did you have a good nap?" I cuddled the baby-bundle in my arms. She yawned softly and blinked up at me. "I'm your Daddy."

She seemed unimpressed as I smoothed a finger across her powder soft cheek. She let out a loud squawk. I wanted to hand her over to her mama for a feed before she woke up her brother.

Faith placed a pillow on her lap to lay the baby for a feed. I still felt slightly awkward as I turned her around in my arms, so she was facing the right direction and handed her over.

"You picked a beautiful name. I love it more now I have an actual little human to own the name."

Faith smiled up at me then. It was a soft, full smile, just short of beaming. "It's weird you saying that, because it's exactly what I've been thinking. I'm loving your choice too, Colter Jace Warner. Although I know he's going to be CJ."

I grinned. "Or Colt."

I felt a swell of love fill my chest as I watched the two ladies I loved the most in my life. Pulling my chair over to the side of the bed close to Faith, I took her free hand into mine and threaded my fingers with hers. She looked up from the baby into my eyes, questioning.

"Before the hordes arrive to see the twins, I want to tell you I love you, Fate. Thank you for making my life, and me, so fulfilled and whole. I always felt like the world wasn't right without you in it, that there was a missing piece of me. I can't imagine how I even survived without you. You are my world ... You and Scott and now these two little precious rewards you gave us."

Faith eyes misted over, and she sent a shaky smile my way. "I never thought I'd have more children." She looked down at the little head nursing at her breast. "It's a miracle. A miracle you helped make happen." She squeezed my hand. "I should be the one thanking you. I love you."

MESSAGE FROM THE AUTHOR

Thank you for reading *'Having Faith.'* I hope you enjoyed reading it, as much as I did writing it. If you did, please consider leaving a review.

Join my Newsletter to find out when my next book will be available.

Watch out for my next story in the 'Mature Love Series' called –

ALL THE DUMB THINGS

You know all those wonderful sayings how 'life dishes out lessons' and 'read the signs' before you act. Yeah well, in matters of love I've subconsciously made it my mission in life to ignore all that great advice.

Instead I'm the person who I'm sure the popular song 'I've Done All the Dumb Things' was written about. I charge in blindly, wearing my heart on my sleeve, only to get it broken. Rinse and repeat.

Maybe I was destined to be this way? My mother's love of Greek Tragedy and Shakespearean Theatre cursing me when she named me Juliet, after the star-crossed lover.

You'd think I'd eventually realise whatever I was doing was wrong. When celebrating my fortieth Birthday the penny finally dropped. I'd have to either give up on love, before it gave up on me.

Only my best friend, Trey, the man I've been secretly in love with for almost my entire life, has other ideas.

ABOUT THE AUTHOR

Georgia Tingley is a new player on the author scene with her breakout novel 'Justice' the first book in the 'Angel Calling' Series.

She loves writing and creating stories so much that it's become her drug of choice and freely confesses to being an addict. After deciding to take on the thrill of writing, she hasn't looked back.

Having lived in various countries while growing up – India, England, Canada, New Zealand and Australia, she calls Western Australia home, living near some of the best beaches in Australia.

In her downtime she loves to read, read and read. Watch TV shows, and movies, do crafts and get into the garden. Swimming and snorkeling are favorite pastimes and she tries to do laps at every opportunity. She and her husband enjoy taking the caravan on trips into the Australian Outback and seeing as much of the 'red' country as they can.

Please feel free to say g'day!

CONTACT INFORMATION

Website: http://georgiatingley.com/

Facebook: https://www.facebook.com/Georgia-Tingley-Author-1744372182538403

Twitter: https://twitter.com/GeorgiaTingley1

Instagram:
https://www.instagram.com/georgiatingley/

Purchase: https://books2read.com/GeorgiaTingley-Author

https://www.amazon.com/s?k=GEORGIA+TINGLEY&ref=nb_sb_noss_2

BOOKS

ANGEL CALLING SERIES

 *JUSTICE* - Book #1

 *AN UNHOLY GIFT* - Book #2

MATURE LOVE SERIES

 *HAVING FAITH*

 *ALL THE DUMB THINGS*

NOVELLA

 *WHISTLER WONDERLAND*